Willow wanted to shake up her life, to be daring. At least for one night...

The perfect partner-in-crime was watching her with bedroom eyes, his face partially hidden by a red devil mask.

In the middle of the dance fl......ghtened, leaning her off center ....p in the back of his ....g her.

There was no........him. He devoured ....manding. Heat and need............, sharp and unexpected. Th...........e slipped in, sliding deliciously again......own.

Tearing them apart, he brought her upright.

She clung to his shoulders, afraid that if she let go she'd topple to the ground.

"Why'd you do that?" she asked breathlessly.

"Because I could. Because I enjoy shaking things up." His deep blue eyes flashed dangerously. "And because I would have kicked myself if I let you go without knowing how your mouth tasted."

Dear Reader,

Long before I met Dev and Willow I knew I wanted to write a story centered around a masquerade. There's something so liberating about donning a mask. It frees you to act wild, be daring and maybe step out of your comfort zone...even if only for a few hours.

I come by my love of costumes honestly. I've been traipsing across the stage since I was a little girl, first as a dancer and then as an actress. My local community theater was a home for me, a place where I belonged. I grew up there, discovering myself as I tried on different personalities and roles to see if they fit.

Though it's been quite a while since I've been in a show, I have managed to find another outlet for my dramatic tendencies. Each year my local Romance Writers of America chapter holds a murder-mystery dinner. And let me just say, we totally embrace the experience. We take on completely different personas...and sometimes even genders. We laugh until we cry and, more often than not, don't even bother solving the mystery.

I hope you enjoy Willow and Dev's story. Maybe they'll inspire you to don a mask and act a little crazy every now and again. I'd love to hear from you at www.kirasinclair.com or come chat with me on Twitter, www.twitter.com/KiraSinclair.

Best wishes,

Kira

The Devil
She Knows

—

Kira Sinclair

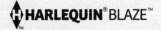

Recycling programs
for this product may
not exist in your area.

ISBN-13: 978-0-373-79770-7

THE DEVIL SHE KNOWS

Copyright © 2013 by Kira Bazzel

This edition published by arrangement with Harlequin Books S.A.

For questions and comments about the quality of this book,
please contact us at CustomerService@Harlequin.com.

® and TM are trademarks of Harlequin Enterprises Limited or its
corporate affiliates. Trademarks indicated with ® are registered in the
United States Patent and Trademark Office, the Canadian Trade Marks
Office and in other countries.

Printed in U.S.A.

ABOUT THE AUTHOR

Kira Sinclair is an award-winning author who writes emotional, passionate contemporary romances. Double winner of the National Readers' Choice Award, her first foray into writing fiction was for a high-school English assignment. Nothing could dampen her enthusiasm...not even being forced to read the love story aloud to the class. However, it definitely made her blush. Writing about striking, sexy heroes and passionate, determined women has always excited her. She lives out her own happily-ever-after with her amazing husband, their two beautiful daughters and a menagerie of animals on a small farm in North Alabama. Kira loves to hear from readers at www.kirasinclair.com.

Books by Kira Sinclair

HARLEQUIN BLAZE
415—WHISPERS IN THE DARK
469—AFTERBURN
588—CAUGHT OFF GUARD
605—WHAT MIGHT HAVE BEEN
667—BRING IT ON*
672—TAKE IT DOWN*
680—RUB IT IN*
729—THE RISK-TAKER
758—SHE'S NO ANGEL

*Island Nights

To get the inside scoop on Harlequin Blaze and its talented writers, be sure to check out blazeauthors.com.

Other titles by this author available in ebook format.
Don't miss any of our special offers. Write to us at the following address for information on our newest releases.

Harlequin Reader Service
U.S.: 3010 Walden Ave., P.O. Box 1325, Buffalo, NY 14269
Canadian: P.O. Box 609, Fort Erie, Ont. L2A 5X3

I'd like to dedicate this book to my amazing, wonderful and brilliant daughters. I'm so proud of the young women you're both growing into.

I hope that one day you'll find friends like Hope, Lexi, Willow and Tatum, and like the friends I'm blessed to have in my life. Women who will listen to you whine, let you cry on their shoulders, rejoice at your triumphs and offer a shovel if someone needs to die...even if only in jest. That kind of solidarity is priceless and absolutely necessary for getting through life with your sanity intact.

I love you both!

1

Sweetheart, South Carolina,
the home of happily-ever-after

DEVLIN WARWICK BLEW past the ornate sign with its elegant gold scrollwork. He didn't bother to hide his curling scowl. Please. The only happily-ever-after he'd ever gotten was the day he'd left town.

Hitting the gas, Dev pushed his shiny red pickup past the speed limit. He watched the needle creep to fifty, sixty and head straight for eighty. He didn't care. He wanted the speed. Let Sheriff Grant pull him over. Unlike the last time they'd tangled, at least the officer would have a legitimate reason to hassle him.

With the windows rolled down and heavy metal cranked loud, Dev enjoyed the anticipation. The citizens of Sweetheart had no idea what was about to hit them. He'd waited a long time for this moment.

He'd left—been run out of town was more like it—ten years earlier with everyone's condemnation ringing in his ears. There was nothing the citizens of Sweetheart hated more than a scandal, although they certainly ate up the gossip that came with it. He'd given them plenty of both.

His grandfather had kicked him out. He'd lost the only family he had left. The irony was that he hadn't actually committed the crime they'd tried and convicted him of in the court of public opinion.

But now he was back. Successful, despite their predictions that he'd end up a drug addict or a felon, just like his dad.

He was going to enjoy this.

Dev pulled into the driveway of his grandfather's house and sat with the motor idling. There was always the inn....

But, he reminded himself, the past didn't live inside these walls. Neither did his grandfather, who'd died four years ago. Dev hadn't even known he was sick.

The darkened windows mocked him, reminding him that he was completely alone. The house was his now, not that he'd seen it since the night he left.

It hadn't changed.

The facade was well maintained, but there were still signs of wear and tear. The house was at least fifty years old and had been well used. No doubt the second stair to the porch still creaked. The shutters needed repainting. Maybe he'd take care of that while he was here.

At least the front landscaping was immaculate. He paid enough money to keep it that way. Trimmed shrubs filled the space behind the stone retaining wall. He'd missed the amazing shade of blue of his grandmother's hydrangeas by a couple of months. No matter how hard he tried, he could never quite get the same color. Her rosebushes in the back might have late blooms, though.

The few memories he had of his grandmother all involved her kneeling on the ground, her hands deep in dirt. For a little boy, furious and lost, the quiet moments they'd shared in the garden had been a lifeline he'd desperately needed.

Unfortunately, those visits had been all too short. The taste of something sweet that had turned bitter because he could never stay longer than a few weeks. When he'd come to live in Sweetheart full time at the age of fifteen his grandma had already been gone.

He had mixed emotions about walking through the dark green front door. The specter of that last night reared its ugly head. Yelling, screaming, his grandfather throwing one of his grandmother's prized figurines at the wall as he ordered Dev out.

Broken pieces of ceramic scattering across the floor. Blood trickling from a nick in his cheek.

Without thought, Dev reached for the scar. The pad of his finger ran down the puckered flesh, a constant reminder of the price he'd paid for something he hadn't even done.

But he'd learned his lesson well. If you were going to get punished for the sin you might as well enjoy committing it.

If only he could manage to hold on to the rage of that night. But if the house held some of his worst memories, it also held the best.

His grandfather, the closest thing he'd had to a father, had patiently taught him how to use power tools in the dusty, dank garage. Together they'd spent countless hours throwing a ball at the hoop tacked to the side of the house. They'd moved silently together in the kitchen as they both attempted, badly, to cook dinner.

When he'd had nowhere else to go his grandfather had taken him in, given him a home and his first taste of tough love. After the kind of mindless liberty he'd known all his life, Sweetheart had been like a prison, full of rules he didn't give a damn about.

His grandfather had expected a lot. The crushing weight of that responsibility had been so constricting, especially when Dev knew he couldn't live up to it.

Better to accept the low expectations and just embrace the inevitable. It was almost a relief when he could let go of the secret hope that this time somehow things would be different. They never were.

At least not back then. Now… After years of hard work he was successful. And low-balling the Sweetheart Consortium's bid for their new resort had been an easy decision. He might lose a little money on the job, but he could afford the hit. And the time away to oversee this project himself.

These days he rarely took on a job personally. He had several managers who normally went to the sites. Lately he'd spent more time in boardrooms than with his hands deep in the earth. Sweetheart was a chance to remedy that…and get a little revenge of the *see how successful I've become* variety.

He was looking forward to the moment when the town realized they'd hired *him*. Watching them squirm was going to be sweet.

It was just his luck that he'd arrived in time for one of the splashy parties Sweetheart loved. The Fall Masquerade would afford him the perfect opportunity to scope things out while keeping his presence a secret.

Tonight he planned to watch and learn. What had changed and who was in charge? How could he exploit the situation to turn the screws on those who'd assumed the worst of him without bothering to actually discover the truth?

Grabbing his garment bag and duffel, Dev finally went inside to change. He might prefer the jeans and work boots he wore when tromping around a site, but he was equally comfortable in the tailored suits required when making presentations to conglomerates and corporations.

The red silk mask was unusual, but it would keep his identity a secret, at least for tonight. And he had to admit he enjoyed the private joke—the top twisted up into two pointy devil horns. The devil among the saints.

Tonight he'd take in the spectacle. Tomorrow he'd get to work. And relish their frustration as the citizens of Sweetheart tried to make his life hell.

The difference between now and ten years ago was that this time there was nothing Sweetheart could take.

A BUZZ OF anticipation and excitement ran through the room. The Fall Masquerade was always a highlight of the year. Everyone loved the chance to dress up and be anonymous for a little while.

Well, everyone except Willow Portis. Despite no one knowing who she was, she felt uncomfortable. Stupid. Waiting for someone to laugh at her costume. Although, so far all she'd gotten were compliments.

"Quick, touch me."

Surprised, Willow stared at the gladiator. The costume would have worked better if he'd had the ripped body to match. "What? Why?"

"So I can tell my friends I've been touched by an angel."

Compliments and bad pickup lines. Willow touched him all right—she shoved the idiot out of her way. Deciding there was safety in numbers, she walked over to the tables set up with refreshments. Her friend Jenna was catering, although Willow hadn't seen her.

Settling for punch, she crossed her arms over her chest and scanned the crowd for a familiar face. Even living in Sweetheart her whole life, and knowing everyone at the party, it was difficult to tell who was behind some of the masks.

Which was exactly what she was counting on—that no one would recognize her.

With nothing better to do, Willow stood and watched, trying to figure out who people were. Tarzan and Jane were clearly Tony and Michelle Sewell. The superhero with them was Wes Unger, Tony's best friend since grade school. The sexy nurse was Carol Ann Kline, a transplanted divorcee, hell-bent on hooking a Sweetheart man.

Distracted by her little game, Willow didn't realize someone was behind her until a long shadow spread across the table. Heavy hands landed on her waist and then ran slowly up her ribs.

She jumped. Her skin crawled. Smacking down on the hands, she stopped them from traveling higher. "What are you doing?"

"Checking for injuries. The fall from heaven must have hurt."

Willow bit back a groan. "Seriously?"

"Trust me, I'm a doctor."

Using the sharp points of her elbows, Willow pushed the guy away from her and turned. Indeed, he was dressed as a doctor, complete with green scrubs, stethoscope and a surgical mask obscuring half his face.

From somewhere deep inside, a fit of pique threatened to take over. The doctor reached for her again, but she held out a hand to stop him. To his credit, he didn't push. He was pissing her off, but he wasn't dangerous, just obnoxious and uncouth.

"If you touch me again, I'm going to make you regret it."

Maybe using a temporary rinse to dye her hair a shocking red had been a bad idea, after all. At the time, covering up her dark, ordinary brown had seemed like a smart move. But combined with the mask that obscured half her face, it seemed to make her unrecognizable. Although it was entirely possible that the dress she'd designed was more responsible for the attention she was getting.

She'd wanted to be daring. To take a risk.

For the past several months, she'd been fighting hard against a restlessness she couldn't explain. Her business was doing well. She had more requests for exclusive wedding gown designs than she had time to fulfill, and stores all around the world had picked up her latest collection. The boutique was thriving. Clients came from all over the South for wedding, bridesmaid and prom dresses—and everything else that went with those important purchases.

After putting herself into debt to open her design company and boutique with Macey, her business partner and friend, the scales had finally started to tip in the past few years.

By most standards she was successful.

So, why did she feel so...lost?

If she was honest with herself she'd admit the disquiet had started when she began designing Hope's wedding dress. It wasn't that she begrudged her friend happiness...it just brought home that she'd spent all of her energy on her business and none on her personal life.

She designed wedding gowns all day, but the prospect of creating her own felt like a dream completely out of reach. The constant barrage of giddy brides searching through their merchandise for that dream dress was getting to her. And if she wasn't careful, the jaded edge she'd developed was going to morph into complete indifference. When that happened, her ability to create magical, romantic and sexy dresses would dry up.

Part of the reason she kept her business in Sweetheart was because of the atmosphere. The entire town was built around the idea that love and marriage could equal lifelong happiness. And her creative process needed that inspiration. She designed dresses for the most important day in any woman's life...she had to believe there was more beyond that day, or the creations would just turn into piles of expensive material and beads with no heart.

It had been a long time since she'd felt desired and sensual in her own skin. So tonight she was taking advantage of the disguise to be daring, something she did not do. She was stepping out on a limb, secure in the knowledge that she could keep her little walk on the wild side a secret.

The masks provided anonymity and freedom. To further confuse everyone, she'd designed a dress she'd never, in the light of day, consider wearing. One of her own sexy, slinky creations paired with two arching angel wings she'd hand-stitched and then laced onto the back of the bodice. Stark white feathers rose behind to tower over her by at least a foot. Instead of wedding white, she'd made the dress out of a pale silvery gray.

The tight bodice, flared mermaid skirt, flowing sleeves and naked shoulders showed off more of her body than she was usually comfortable with. Willow had worked hard to build the image of a quiet, accomplished businesswoman. She clung to it, wrapping the familiar shield around her. Flaunting her body went against years of trying to live down the scandal of her sister's disgrace.

Rose had always worn the smallest, tightest things she could get away with. She'd stayed out all night, drunk excessively and embraced everything their parents had warned her to avoid. Everyone had hoped her older sister would outgrow her penchant for pushing boundaries and making mistakes, especially when she eloped with an older man who had an established, settled life. Perhaps his love would be enough to curb her destructive behavior.

Unfortunately, it wasn't.

Not only hadn't he settled her, he'd been betrayed by Rose in the worst way. Then, after the divorce, her sister had headed as far as she could get from Sweetheart, taking the settlement and becoming a showgirl in Sin City. Willow cringed every time she thought of Rose on stage, topless in front of thousands of strangers. But Rose refused to cash the checks Willow sent, insisting she didn't need the help.

Forcing the unhappy thoughts away, Willow realized maybe it was inevitable that Rose would pop up in her mind tonight. Even as she'd put the dress and mask on, part of her had felt as if she was betraying the reputation she'd fought hard to build.

Needing a break from the blatant sexual come-ons, Willow worked her way into the corner. It was her default position for these types of events. Having the solid support of the wall behind her was comforting and familiar.

She was seriously considering calling it a night when her friend Tatum, the local florist who had designed the amazing red, orange and yellow centerpieces, sidled up beside her.

"Do I want to know what prompted this little outfit?"

Willow cut wary eyes to her friend. If any of their group would understand, it would be Tatum. She was a no-nonsense, make-no-apologies kind of person. Willow admired her for that self-confidence. Tatum didn't need anyone's approval.

After spending her entire life worrying what others thought, Willow was envious. But she had no idea how to adopt Tatum's cavalier attitude. It just wasn't her.

"What do you mean?" she asked, still uncertain if Tatum knew who she was. She hadn't told any of her friends what she'd planned to do tonight. She'd been apprehensive about their reactions. She wasn't interested in being razzed for the decision…or talked out of it.

Tatum's pale green eyes raked Willow from the tip of her head to the toe of the designer heels peeking out beneath her hem.

"Well, let's start with the hair. I really hope it's temporary. While I'm all for taking a risk, you've never struck me as a red kinda girl. And the dress. Don't misunderstand, it's gorgeous—how could it not be? You designed it—but a little revealing for you, isn't it?"

Oh, Tatum knew it was her. "Thanks, Mom."

Her friend chuckled, sipped on the glass of punch she held. "Don't get me wrong. If you really want to go there, I'll support you one hundred percent. But as long as I've known you, this—" her hand waved up and down to take in Willow's entire ensemble "—has never been your thing."

Tatum turned, giving her back to the room and blocking out everyone else. Her stare was serious and sharp. "I've had my fair share of one-night-stand regrets. I just want to make sure you know what you're getting yourself into."

Willow shook her head. "No one said anything about a one-night stand."

"Please, honey, that dress screams 'screw me.' Right along with the underlying air of innocence that not even your amazing creation can completely cover up. You're like catnip, and every single man here is sniffing."

Willow wanted to dismiss her friend's observation—she wasn't catnip for anyone—but the barrage of bad lines she'd heard tonight had her swallowing the words.

"Right now, there are at least six men who can't take their eyes off you."

"How do you know? Your back is to the room."

Tatum shrugged. "What do I always do at these things? I've been watching. The real question is, what are *you* going to do about it?"

"What do you mean?"

"Are you going to stay here in the corner, or are you going to get out there and flirt?" Shifting to stand beside her, Tatum crossed her arms over her chest, leaned against the wall and stared into the pulsing crowd. Tatum hated these things, and still she always came.

"Corner," Willow answered without a second thought.

"I'm not sure he's going to be satisfied with that answer." Without bothering to look, Tatum tipped her head sideways.

Willow followed the gesture, her eyes scanning the crowd for whatever her friend was talking about.

And then she saw him.

Even from behind the barrier of his red-satin devil mask, she could feel the intensity of his stare as it ran slowly over her body. And she reacted. Her body buzzed with the recognition of a virile, interested male.

Through the space and the shield of his mask she couldn't tell the color of his eyes, but they were dark. People brushed past him on both sides. The cacophony of voices and music swirled between them. Someone bumped his shoulder. But he didn't move. None of the chaos touched him.

Willow's throat went dry. Her pulse fluttered uncomfortably. She wanted to look away, but couldn't.

Then he moved. Toward her. Willow reached for

Tatum, hoping to use her as a deflection, but her friend had disappeared. Damn her.

Dressed all in black, the only colors he wore were the shocking red mask and a slate-gray tie. Willow recognized expensive material and tailoring when she saw it. His suit hugged him perfectly, highlighting the beautiful body beneath.

Whoever he was, he had money. Not that Willow particularly cared about that.

"Like to dance?" He held out his hand, palm up.

Willow stared at it for several seconds, torn. Slowly, her gaze traveled up his body to his eyes. They were a dark, midnight-blue.

Licking her lips, she said, "That's all?"

"That isn't enough?"

"Every other guy here has had some cheesy line about angels or sin."

"You're too intelligent for that."

"How do you know?"

During the entire exchange he held his hand steady between them, waiting. There was a…stillness inside him. A patience she instinctively recognized. He'd show that same patience in bed as he drove her crazy with precision and skill.

Willow fought the urge to squirm. She found herself nodding but didn't reach for him, vacillating between what she wanted to do and what she should do. She wanted to let this handsome, dynamic and mysterious man sweep her off her feet. And he so could. Her skin tingled. Her body fizzed with anticipation.

But what she should do was turn around and walk away. Everything inside her told her that was the smart, responsible, correct response. Years of doing the right thing and choosing the safe course were hard to ignore.

Good habits were just as hard to break as the bad ones.

But tonight she'd come here to be daring, to do something different and shake up her life. At least for one night.

The perfect opportunity to do that stared at her with dark, sensual, bedroom eyes.

2

APPARENTLY TIRED OF waiting for her to make up her mind, the devil took the decision from her. Wrapping an arm around her waist, he pulled her tight against his body and led her to the center of the dance floor.

Languid heat spread through her when his palm slipped down her spine, ruffling feathers as he went, to settle at the small of her back. Bringing her close, he flattened her other hand against his chest and engulfed it in his own.

Was it an accident that she could feel the accelerated thrum of his heart against her palm?

Rough stubble scraped her temple. The heavy beat of the music slipped into her blood, settling as a steady and agonizing vibration deep in her belly.

Moist heat tickled across her cheek when he said, "I'm Dev."

"Willow."

His entire body hardened. His back stiffened and the pectoral muscle beneath their joined hands turned to stone. She didn't understand and tried to pull back, but his tight hold on her waist wouldn't let her.

Desperate to find some way to ease the tension, Willow licked her lips and said, "You aren't from here."

Gradually, his body relaxed, although she could still feel the tight muscles beneath her hands. With relief, her body melted into him.

She didn't want him to pull away.

He'd barely touched her, and her skin felt hot enough to flame right off her body. Every nerve ending was alive with anticipation. Every shift of his body against hers registered deep inside. The friction was unbearable. Never in her life had she been this…inundated by her physical response to a man. To a stranger.

She couldn't breathe. She couldn't think. All she could do was want. Him.

"Why do you say that?"

"Because I know everyone and I don't know you."

A deep rumbling sound rolled through his chest. It reverberated straight into her, making her internal muscles pulse and ache.

Around them, the people faded away. Willow couldn't concentrate on anything but the sensations bombarding her. The music changed. He put more space between them. She wanted to protest, to grab him back and close the gap.

But she didn't.

The dark, earthy scent of him washed over her and she liked it. Pine, soil, wood. Unlike men who relied on something artificial, he was all musky, sinful, primitive male.

The pad of his thumb ran across the center of her

palm and up the underside of her left ring finger. Goose bumps erupted up her arm.

"You aren't married?"

"No."

"You sure?"

"I think I'd remember something like that. I hope."

Dev chuckled softly against her temple. "What do you do?"

"I'm a wedding-gown designer."

"That explains the dress."

Willow frowned. "What's that supposed to mean?"

The dimple at the center of his chin twitched. The thick stubble on his face almost obscured it. Almost, but not quite. Willow wanted to touch. To put her tongue right there and taste.

Holy crap, what was this man doing to her?

"This dress is hardly a costume. It stands out."

It was Willow's turn to stiffen beneath his hold.

"In a good way," he quickly assured her. "Everyone else's costume is a cheap imitation of yours." His mouth found her ear. "I recognize quality and appreciate it when I get my hands on it."

A shiver rippled through her. As close as they were, there was no way he hadn't felt her reaction. Willow fought the tide of embarrassment.

Closing her eyes, she tried to find some self-control. She was usually so good at suppressing her reactions— to everything. But this man seemed to have a knack for breaking through all of her armor as if it didn't even exist. Only one other man had ever affected her that way....

"Don't."

"Don't what," she asked, her voice breaking on the words.

"Don't hide."

"I'm not."

"You are. My little angel, pulling the edges of her virtue back around her. Why? Are you worried about what these people will think?"

His dark, glittering gaze darted around the room to encompass the crush of people surrounding them. For the first time, Willow realized they'd become the center of attention. Other people twirled, talked, drank and ate…but eyes kept straying back to the angel and devil pressed against each other.

God, she hoped no one realized she was the one making a spectacle of herself. Her costume was good, but was it that good? Tatum had known who she was.

"Yes. I live here." These people were her neighbors, her friends, her customers. Of course she cared what they thought. She'd seen firsthand just how cruel they could be.

She didn't want that for herself. Would do just about anything to avoid the agony of losing their respect. Losing her own respect.

"So you do. Do you think these people have never sinned?"

"Of course I don't."

"Then why do you have to be perfect?"

"I'm not."

He stopped. In the middle of the dance floor. His arms tightened, leaning her off center. His gaze bored into hers, searching for something. She couldn't breathe. She didn't want to.

Her lips parted anyway, trying to pull more oxygen into her lungs. He made a sound deep in the back of his throat. His body loomed over hers, dangerous and tempting.

And then he was kissing her.

There was no easing into the moment, not with him. He devoured her, his mouth hard and demanding. She couldn't say no. Didn't really want to. The undertow of sensation pulled at her, blocking out every other thing.

Willow's eyes closed. The bank of revolving lights flashed colors across her lids. And she held on. It was the only thing she could do.

Heat and need twisted through her, sharp and unexpected. She didn't know what to do with it. His tongue slipped in, sliding deliciously against her own. The texture and taste of him was extreme. He'd sampled the cheap champagne someone had provided, fruity and sharp, but underneath he was rugged and robust.

Tearing away, Dev pulled her upright. The room spun lazily as she tried to get her bearings.

She blinked up at him. And then blinked again. Her hands clung to his shoulders, holding tight for fear that if she let go she'd topple to the ground.

"Why'd you do that?" she asked breathlessly.

"Because I could. Because I enjoy making a stir." His deep blue eyes flashed dangerously. "Because I would have kicked myself if I let you go without knowing how your mouth tasted."

No one had ever said anything that…sensual to her. "Holy hell."

The startled sound of his laughter burst between them. Had she said that out loud?

Willow stared at him, surprised by his reaction. She wanted to see his face. To know what his laughter looked like. Would it lighten the shadows cast by more than the mask covering him?

Wrapping his arms around her shoulders, Dev pulled her tight to his body. The embrace had none of the underlying currents of sensuality and need from moments before. It was easy and let her relax.

"Thank you," he said, his mouth buried against the feathers of her mask.

"For what?"

"For giving me a moment to remember in the middle of all this. I didn't expect that when I arrived tonight. Didn't expect you."

Willow wasn't entirely certain what to make of that. "You're welcome?"

Spinning her once more and setting her off center, he asked, "Do you want to leave?"

Without hesitating, Willow answered, "Yes." This man with the dark blue eyes and red-silk mask was precisely what she'd been looking for when she'd dressed tonight.

It was finally her turn to sin.

FROM ACROSS THE room Dev watched Willow Portis as she spoke to a woman in a halfhearted cat costume. The two women couldn't have been more different. Willow was long and slender. Not even her blatant attempts at the sexy costume could hide her inherent elegance. Her movements were deliberate, not a single motion wasted.

He shouldn't have been surprised to find her at the masquerade, but he was. Maybe because he knew her sister and parents had moved away from Sweetheart. He'd always imagined her living somewhere else, with the perfect life.

From the moment he'd walked into the party she'd drawn his gaze. His, and that of every red-blooded male in the room. When he'd first approached her it had simply been because he was attracted and interested in learning more about the woman beneath the sexy dress and virginal angel wings.

He should have known who she was the moment he touched her, but it hadn't been until she told him her name that realization—and long-forgotten memories—flooded in.

Part of him wondered just how long it would take her to recognize him. How far was she willing to go with this? And would she push him away when she figured it out or take the opportunity to finish what they'd started ten years ago?

Would she still hate him? Blame him? Or would time have blunted the misplaced sense of betrayal?

Some perverse place deep inside him wanted to know...what had her life become? Why was she here tonight alone? How had she spent the past ten years? And was she happy?

Even as he realized he should probably walk away from her, he couldn't make himself do it. Just as before. From the moment he'd met her, there'd been something about Willow that had drawn him in. Made him want things he knew he couldn't have.

Her sweet and haughty demeanor was a dichotomy that had intrigued him from the moment Rose had introduced them. Even back then he'd wanted to ruffle her feathers, to make her cool skin pink with a blush of innocence.

Until Willow, he hadn't known innocence still existed. Dealing with his mother's alternating rampages and drug-induced bouts of euphoria had stolen his innocence long before he'd come to Sweetheart.

She'd been seventeen to his twenty. And though he'd known he should leave her alone, he hadn't been able to do it. Every time she was close, the need to fluster her was overwhelming. He'd push into her personal space and watch as her body reacted to him—as he knew she didn't want it to.

Just like everyone else in Sweetheart, she was a bit condescending. But that had only made him want her more. To prove that she was no better than anyone else…no better than him.

He'd convinced himself Willow Portis was a challenge, a puzzle he wanted to crack. But it had been more than that. He'd needed to understand. And maybe let her innocence touch him so that he could feel it again just for a little while.

And after months of effort, he'd finally started to win her over. He'd even begun to think that she saw more to him than the rest of the world did—more than the hopeless son of a convicted felon and a drug addict.

Then the debacle with her sister had hit, and everything had gone to hell.

The way she'd looked at him, her eyes filled with betrayal instead of the soft hope he'd come to expect, had hurt more than anything else.

Until she'd been in his arms tonight Dev had honestly thought he'd left the past far behind. But perhaps there was one last thing he had to deal with....

He still wanted Willow with a need so sharp it ground into his bones. Maybe, just maybe, tonight would give him the chance to exorcise those ghosts for good.

"Wick."

The small voice, old nickname and arms flung around his chest startled him. He stumbled back, taking the weight of the woman who'd launched herself at him as if she were an air-hockey puck.

"Erica," she said, burying her face into his shoulder. "Erica Condon." Then she pulled away again, staring up at him with hero worship in her eyes. It made him uncomfortable. "What are you doing here? I didn't realize you were back in town."

Dev threw a hasty glance around the room, grateful that everyone appeared too preoccupied to pay attention. He wasn't ready for his cover to be blown. Not yet. Not when things were just getting interesting.

How the heck had this woman recognized him when Willow hadn't?

Wrapping a hand around her upper arm, he dragged her deeper into the shadows close to the door.

Gently, he disentangled their bodies, putting several inches between them. "Look, I have no idea who you are." Maybe if her costume hadn't been so distracting and unflatteringly psychedelic...

Hurt and surprise washed across her face making him feel guilty. Trying to blunt the harshness of his words, he offered her a smile. "I'd like to keep my presence quiet, at least for tonight."

She nodded eagerly. And that's when recognition hit.

She'd been Rose's best friend. He'd never understood
what had drawn the two girls together. Erica had been
short, quiet and shy. Rose was gregarious and effer-
vescent. On the surface, the two didn't match. Secretly
Dev had always thought Erica's eagerness to please had
been why Rose kept her around.

She hadn't fit into the crowd he and Rose had run
with. They'd all been wild and adventurous. Erica had
been the quiet girl that everyone sort of ignored. Dev
cringed, feeling guilty for the way he'd dismissed her
when he was younger.

That guilt might have kept him talking with her, but
when he glanced away to find Willow walking through
the crowd toward them everything else faded away. She
was dynamically gorgeous. His body hardened with the
immediate need to touch her. To taste her. To know her
in a way he'd been denied before.

The tight cut of her dress left her little choice but to
take measured steps, constricting her movements and
giving him a perfect view of her sinuous body as she
moved.

Several men turned to watch her cut through the
crowd. Dev recognized the heat and purpose deep in
their eyes, knew his own burned with the same appreciation. An unbidden growl rolled through his chest.
Tossing some random words over his shoulder, he left
Erica gape-mouthed and headed straight for Willow.

No one else was getting close to her. Tonight, she
was his. Finally.

He understood the gazes she drew, like iron filings
to a magnet, the force of her unavoidable. The need to
kiss her again, right here, right now, in front of every

other male, broke deep inside. He resisted. Not only wouldn't it matter, but Willow wouldn't appreciate a repeat performance of the public display.

She was still a walking contradiction.

The dress labeled her a siren. But the way her body had trembled when he'd pulled her close to dance, her wary expression and the hesitation in her touch told him a different story.

Her sister's lies had taken everything from him—including Willow. He'd worked for years to rebuild his life and feel comfortable in his own skin.

She stopped in front of him, staring up through inky-black lashes and blue eyes that were bright and deep. The skin of her shoulders, left bare by her dress, was milky-white and perfectly matched the feathers that arched from either side of her shoulder blades.

He wanted to touch, to run the pad of his finger across her skin to see if it was as smooth and delicate as it looked.

But he didn't.

The enticing pink tip of her tongue darted out to nervously wet her bottom lip.

"Take me to bed."

The mask shielded some of her expression, so he couldn't tell if she was as surprised by her own proposition as he was. That was not what he'd expected to come out of her mouth. He'd actually been waiting for an excuse, for her to come to her senses and realize the danger of what she was doing.

Did she already know who he was? Was she taking advantage of the opportunity fate had plopped into their laps?

"If you want to, that is." Her voice quivered.

"I'd be an idiot if I didn't." Something, possibly the integrity he'd fought hard to rediscover, made him ask, "Are you sure?"

She swallowed and took a single step closer. Slowly, her gaze rolled up to his. Her chin followed until she was looking him square in the eye.

The impact of her stare hit him like a fist. What he saw made every muscle in his body tighten. Pure, un-adulterated hunger. It called to him. It stirred something deep inside that had been dormant for years.

"I haven't been this sure about anything in a long while."

3

NERVES CHURNED IN Willow's belly. Ensconced in her own car, the red pickup keeping pace behind her, she had plenty of opportunity to second-guess herself. Maybe she should tell Dev she'd changed her mind.

But the moment they arrived at her home and he stepped from the large red truck, she couldn't find the words.

Instead she blurted out, "That's not what I expected," nodding to the intimidating vehicle behind him.

Heavy lids slid down over glowing blue eyes. The left side of his mouth quirked up into a half smile. He stalked closer. "What were you expecting?"

Reaching for the lapels of his suit, Willow let her fingers run up and down the expensive material. It was soft against her skin. She loved the subtle texture of it. Touching it settled her as nothing else probably could have.

She looked up into his shrouded eyes, still obscured by the mask he was wearing, and the butterflies that had taken up residence in her stomach disappeared. She wanted this. She wanted him.

For once she was going to be daring and take what she wanted. Tomorrow would be soon enough to worry about the aftermath.

"Something low and sleek. Fast. Dangerous. Gunmetal-gray, like your tie." She let her hand slip down the silky line before tugging at the knot to loosen it.

"What an imagination you have. This is a costume. That—" he gestured negligently behind him at the hulking red truck parked in her driveway "—is real."

Her fingers trailed over the cut of his suit. "This is no costume. I know expensive hand tailoring when I see it."

She watched as a sheepish grin touched his lips. "All right, I do have a Jag sitting in the garage at home. But it's also red, so I don't think that counts."

"Oh, it counts." She touched the mask covering his face and then glanced at the truck. "Have a thing for red, do you?"

He ran a finger down her hair. Tingles shattered across her scalp. "Maybe."

Trusting he would follow, Willow walked into her home. Leaving the door open, she dropped her clutch on the table by the door and threw her keys into the bowl she kept there. The soft click of the lock catching sent a jolt of need through her.

She closed her eyes for a brief moment. His fingers slipped down the curve of her neck. Her skin pebbled in response to his caress.

"Would you like a glass of wine?" Did she want him to say yes or did she want him to say no?

"What I want is you." His voice was close, closer

than she'd expected. "To kiss you here." His fingers trailed across her shoulders. "And here." His touch continued down her spine. Not even the barrier of her dress could prevent the heat of him from seeping deep inside.

His arm circled her body, pulling her tight against him. Her back pressed into his chest. Her head fell against his shoulder. Feathers arced out from between them, tickling her cheek.

He drew a line down the center of her body, through the valley between her breasts, across her stomach and to the juncture of her thighs. "And here. I want to know the sound you make when you let go. I want the taste of you on my tongue."

"Yes," she breathed out. She'd never wanted anything more.

Dev took a step back. She felt the loss of him immediately. She tried to turn, but the weight of his hands on her shoulders held her in place.

Gently, he found the complicated laces that connected her wings to the dress. She'd built loops into the back panel to keep them from drooping.

Willow hadn't realized the weight of them until they were gone. It was a relief. Several of the feathers escaped, fluttering to the floor around them.

Irrefutable evidence that this angel has truly fallen, she thought.

But when his mouth touched the curve of her neck, Willow couldn't find the desire to care. Not when sinning with this man felt so good.

Talented fingers found the zipper at the back of her dress. The rasp of it echoed through her darkened house.

The sound mingled with her rapid breaths. He'd barely touched her, and she was undone.

Instead of letting the dress fall heavily to the floor as she'd expected, he held it up. As he tugged the sleeves off, one at a time, his mouth found the curve of her neck and sucked.

And then he was at her feet. "Step out," he ordered.

Her hands curled around his shoulders, holding on as she did. Just above the edge of her stocking, the rough stubble of his jaw brushed against the outside of her thigh. But before she could enjoy the sensation, he was on his feet again and walking away. With her dress in his hands.

Willow turned to watch as he draped it carefully over a chair. When he was satisfied, he spun back to her. "That dress is too beautiful to leave in a puddle on the floor."

If that statement had come from any other man she would have worried. But Dev was too masculine and inherently sexual for the words to be anything but a show of consideration for her creation and hard work.

The last of her doubts fled.

From across the room the heat of his dark gaze raked her body. She'd never been so grateful for beautiful underwear in her life.

Because the foundation garments that went under her dresses were just as important as the fit of the gowns, Willow insisted on selling lingerie for the brides. And because she knew that new husbands would be seeing them, she also demanded that the pieces be lovely, sensual and enticing.

The benefit of selling the stuff was getting to take home the pieces she fell in love with. Beautiful lingerie was a secret weakness of hers. Something that she could keep to herself. Although tonight she was happy to share.

His eyes feasted on her. "*That* is unexpected."

"What?"

The merry widow was white and made of see-through mesh and lace. It was strapless; the cups and boning kept it in place. The edge skimmed right at the curve of her hips and a cutout in front showcased matching panties. Tiny iridescent beads edged the lace, and delicate garters stretched down her thighs.

With deliberate steps Dev crossed the room. He stopped before her, but didn't touch. At least, not with anything more than his gaze.

"I didn't think anything could top the dress. I was wrong. I almost wish you still had the wings."

Overwhelmed, Willow dropped her focus to the ground between them.

"Don't." The single growling word startled her into looking back up.

"Don't what?"

"Don't go all virginal on me."

Something about the way he said the word *virginal* pissed her off. He was…annoyed.

This time, she was the one to close the space between them. Grabbing the tie she'd already loosened, Willow pulled him tight against her half-naked body. The texture of his suit touching her skin only served to remind her that she was vulnerable while he was still completely covered up.

He could have stopped her, but he didn't. Instead, he let her pull him down, his back arching so they were face-to-face.

"Don't let the white fool you. I haven't been a virgin since I was sixteen."

The dark wing of his eyebrows rose in surprise. "That young?"

"Let's just say it was a moment of weakness."

"Like me."

"Not like you. That was a regrettable bow to peer pressure and was hardly earth-shattering. This is a moment of insanity. And I have a feeling I'll remember it for the rest of my life. For much better reasons."

"God, I hope so."

"God has nothing to do with it."

Without warning, Dev swept her up into his arms.

She directed him to her bedroom, and he carried her up the stairs as if she was as light as one of the feathers that lay scattered in their wake. He didn't bother to turn on lights when he reached her room. There was enough moonlight that he could see. Placing her softly on the bed, Dev took a step back.

Willow leaned up on her elbows to watch.

Without a care for his own clothes, he let the suit coat slide to the floor. She almost protested, but her mouth was too dry. Anticipation buzzed through her, an electrical shock of need. With dexterous fingers, he finished the job she'd started outside and pulled the tie free.

Without breaking eye contact, he torturously unbuttoned his shirt. Her legs scissored restlessly on the bed, silk rasping against silk. She wanted him to be the one touching her. But she wanted to enjoy the show more.

And she wasn't disappointed. Billowing behind him, the shirt fluttered to the floor, his own set of broken wings.

What to look at first? His chest was wide, shoulders tight with muscle. They tapered down in a V to his amazing abs. His biceps flexed. Jesus, the man was built. And not with the kind of muscles that came from working out in a gym.

What the heck did he do? And why did she care? She could ask him later.

Bouncing up onto her knees, Willow couldn't keep her hands to herself anymore. Grasping the waistband of his pants, she tugged him to the edge of the bed. His hands tangled in her hair, sending the pins she'd used to pull it up scattering across the bed.

Some of them pulled, but she didn't care. Dev's fingers sifted through the strands, combing until all the pins were gone and her hair hung in a waterfall down her back.

He reached for his mask, but she stopped him. His hand stilled beneath hers, a question in his eyes.

"Leave it."

She wanted the masks tonight. She wanted the anonymity they provided and the safety to be and do whatever she wanted without the niggling voice in the back of her head that said she would regret this. Yes, the cover was a ruse and they both knew it, but she needed it.

Without it she wouldn't have the strength to break her own rules.

"All right. If you'll leave these on," he countered,

running a finger down the inside of her thigh to the band of lace circling the top of her stocking.

"Done."

His mouth crushed to hers. He was all sweltering sin. He tasted dark and dangerous. But she opened for him anyway, letting him in. His tongue stroked hers, coaxing and teasing. He sucked, pulling her into his own mouth.

While she was distracted, he was busy disengaging each of the tiny hooks that ran up the length of her spine. The boning fell away. Willow let out a gasp of relief that he swallowed.

Blood rushed to the surface of her skin. His hands scraped down her exposed body, taking advantage of the increased sensitivity. The muscles in her stomach leaped beneath his touch.

But he wasn't the only industrious one. Spreading the fly of his pants open, Willow went searching for what she wanted most. And she wasn't disappointed. Hot and hard, the length of his sex pressed eagerly against her palm.

Talented fingers tugged at her distended nipples. He rolled them, making her ache, and then his thumbs feathered lightly across the sensitive peaks. Willow clenched her thighs together, trying to find some relief, but there wasn't any. At least, none without him.

The need for him spiraled out of control. She shoved his pants to the floor and resented the time it took for him to step out of them because that meant he wasn't touching her.

She bit his shoulder and he sucked in a harsh breath.

In retaliation, he grasped her around the thighs, brought them close together and then pushed her backward.

The pull of gravity was exhilarating. Her entire world tipped off-center. And he was right there with her.

Silk-clad thighs slid slowly up his ribs. Dev settled heavily against the V of her open legs. He felt so good there.

His mouth found her breast and he sucked. The moist heat of him had her arching off the bed.

The rip of fabric tore through the room. A cool gust of air touched her sex. She didn't care. If it meant he'd touch her then he could ruin every last pair of panties she owned. Hell, she'd sew more.

And then he found her. His fingers slipped through her sex, diving deep. She groaned with the bliss of his touch. He found her hidden spot and stroked. Over and over, until she was delirious with the need for more.

Her hands played mindlessly across his body, the pleasure of touching him increasing her own. He was solid and real. Hers to enjoy. Her mouth rained down kisses on every inch of skin she could reach.

Blindly, she fumbled in the bedside table for the box she kept there, not that she needed it often. Grabbing a condom, she used her teeth to open it and then rolled the tight latex over his pulsing hardness.

She wanted him inside her. Now.

Understanding her unspoken urgency, Dev gave her exactly what she wanted. Rearing back, he brought them together, positioning the swollen head of his erection at the aching opening of her sex.

Slowly, he pushed inside, letting her take him inch by inch. He stretched and filled her. His breath came in short gasps as he slid all the way home. His body trembled. She could feel the tremor straight to her center.

He was everywhere. Surrounding her. Over her. Deep inside. His hips flexed against her, drawing a moan and giving her just a little more.

And then he was moving. With slow, deliberate strokes, he pulled out and then thrust back again. Her hips pumped in time with his. He drove her crazy, bringing her to the brink only to push inside and stay there, motionless, while she writhed.

Every muscle in her body was wound tight. Every nerve ending quivered, waiting for the moment when her world would finally break apart.

When it came, the release hit with a force she'd never experienced before. Was it Dev, or was it the edge of danger? She didn't know and didn't care. Everything went black, the tiny bursts of color across her eyelids the only thing in her universe. That and the spot where they joined. The relentless waves of satisfaction.

The frenzy of his release pierced the fog. He thrust into her, his entire body bowing back with tension right before the snap. And then he was calling her name, a guttural groan that echoed deep inside her.

Watching him let go was beautiful, and she wished she'd let him take off the mask so she could see more. See all of him. Before, it had felt right, the barrier she'd kept in place. Now, after what they'd just shared, it felt wrong to have anything between them.

Her body pulsed. Pleasure and something more fizzled through her veins. He collapsed beside her. Willow's body quivered, a spent mess.

Their legs tangled together, but she was too drained

to try to unravel the knot. His arm, draped across her waist, tightened to pull her closer.

"You are definitely no angel."

HE WAS IN serious trouble.

Dev stared down at Willow as she slept. He couldn't settle. His conscience wouldn't let him. What had he done?

She was going to be pissed when she realized who he was. And, really, he wouldn't blame her. But the moment he'd followed her inside…he'd been lost.

The sight of her standing in the dark hallway, moonlight falling across her pale skin and those wings…he'd had to touch. And once his fingers slipped across her smooth skin he couldn't stop.

When she'd told him to keep the masks on he'd been relieved…and guilty as hell. He knew, without a doubt, that the moment she saw his face that would be the end of it. And he'd waited to touch her for so long.

But that didn't change the fact that he'd royally screwed up. It had been a very long time since he'd let his dick do his thinking. Damn thing tended to get him into serious trouble. The question was, how to fix this? If that was even possible.

With a sigh, Willow rolled onto her side. The skin between her eyes crinkled. Then she burrowed into his prostrate body and her entire face smoothed out into sleepy contentment.

Oh, yeah, he was in deep shit.

Her shocking-red hair spread across the pillow. Staring down at her, Dev was careful not to pull as he threaded his fingers through it. He wanted to know what it would look like without the artificial color. His memory of her told him it should be a deep, rich brown that reminded him of fertile, fresh-tilled soil.

She smelled so good. Pressing his nose close to the exposed crook of her neck, he breathed her in. Something soft, sweet and subtle, like honeysuckle on a perfect summer morning.

He wanted more.

And that was really the crux of the problem. One night with her wasn't enough. But when she realized who he was…

The thought of that conversation had dread tightening his gut.

He had two choices. He could leave now and avoid the issue all together. Play this off as the one-night stand she probably thought she'd just had. But that really wasn't going to work for him. Not only did he not want to leave, but he couldn't avoid the confrontation.

Eventually she was going to see him in town and realize who she'd had amazing sex with.

Or he could stay. Brazen it out and try to convince her that he hadn't set out to take advantage of her. That screwing her hadn't been about revenge, but heat and long-denied attraction.

Sliding down, he tucked her body tighter, enjoying the way she fit perfectly against him. Her hair was still clutched in his fist, an unconscious attempt to hold on to what he fully expected to lose.

Had she dyed it for the costume or did she keep it red all the time? He hoped it was temporary. It didn't suit her. At all. Not that it was bad…it just wasn't Willow. Or at least, the Willow he remembered.

Although why he thought he understood her at all he didn't know. Ten years was a long time. He was proof of that. Look at how different he was from the rebellious and angry boy he'd been.

God, he'd been a prick when he'd moved to Sweetheart, defiantly wearing the label on his sleeve. Consumed with pain he didn't want anyone to see. His mom, a drug addict who'd only cared about her next fix, had died from an overdose. He'd been the one to find her pale body, lifeless and cold. And even if she'd been a shitty mother…she'd been his. And it had hurt.

Everyone looked at him and judged. The other kids he went to school with. The teachers who should have been a source of knowledge and help, but were too busy to notice he was lost. Although, it really hadn't been their fault. It wasn't like he was ever around long enough for anyone to put the pieces together.

Dev had lost count how many times his family had been evicted because neither parent could hold a job or bother to pay rent. Moving from place to place meant school to school. After his dad went to jail there'd been several months he hadn't bothered going to class at all. And no one had noticed.

Before Sweetheart he'd never really had a home. A roof over his head, sure. Not a home. But his grandfather had given him one…at least for a little while.

No matter how long he'd lived there, he'd never quite let himself relax. Five years in one place was unheard of for him. And he just kept waiting for it to end. It was almost a relief, when the look in his grandfather's eyes changed from exasperated love to enraged disappointment and the fairy tale was finally over.

Once again, everyone had judged him, looking for the worst and finding only what they expected.

But they'd all been wrong. Sure, he'd floundered for a few months trying to find a way through the mess he'd landed in. Who would have known that picking up an odd job on a construction site could change his life so drastically? He'd never forget the man who'd given him a chance and seen beneath the grimy exterior to the potential lurking deep inside.

He'd gone back to school, finished his degree, and started Devlin Landscaping & Design. At any given time he had hundreds of people working for him all over the country.

Willow had lived in the world he'd wanted desperately to be a part of, but couldn't quite believe he had the right to. She'd been different. Or so he'd thought. But in the end, she'd pushed him away just like his grandfather, easily believing the lies.

Once he might have known the sound of her laughter and the way her eyes darkened when she was angry, but that obviously wasn't enough.

He should probably feel remorse for what he'd just done, but he couldn't muster up the emotion. It would mean he regretted tonight, and he didn't. Maybe he would later, when the piper had to be paid, but for the moment the satisfaction was too close to the surface.

Trouble would find him soon enough, anyway. It always did. Besides, with her naked body pressed close he wanted another taste. There was no point asking for absolution if he fully intended to sin again.

He hadn't gone to that party with the intention of picking someone up. Considering what had happened, sleeping with anyone his first day back in Sweetheart was probably the worst decision he could have made. The fact that it had been Willow just compounded the stupidity.

She really was nothing like her sister, which was a good thing. Rose had been provoking and selfish, caring about no one but herself. Willow was soft and quiet. Giving. Reserved, even if tonight she had wanted to pretend she was daring.

But, God, beneath all the polished restraint she was passionate. And nothing like the women he normally connected with.

He liked to get down and dirty, in his job, in bed and in general. Life was too short and too much shit happened. Shit that no one could predict or control.

So tonight he was going to enjoy the moment. Tomorrow would be soon enough to deal with the rest.

4

WILLOW WOKE SLOWLY, a delicious smile curving her lips before she'd even opened her eyes. Stretching, her body protested in the strangest places.

And then she remembered.

She sat bolt upright, clutching the lavender sheet to her naked chest.

"Oh, my God," she breathed out to the empty room.

It hadn't been a dream. She'd really been that wanton and unabashedly reckless.

Her face flamed with delayed embarrassment. The things she'd done…and let him do to her.

With a groan, she dropped back into the pile of pillows, shielding her face with her arm.

Was it a good thing that she was alone? Or should she be pissed that he'd left while she was asleep? Maybe she should call Tatum and ask her just what morning-after protocol called for.

Memories of last night flashed across her closed lids. A dark head between her open thighs as pleasure spiraled ruthlessly through her. Silky strands clutched between her demanding hands as she kept him right where she wanted him.

His body sliding sinuously against hers in a relentless rhythm that drove her crazy.

Her body hummed, electrified by nothing more than the ghosts of what they'd done to each other and the lingering scent of sex that still clung to her skin.

"Well, that's certainly a nice vision to walk in on."

With a startled yelp, Willow jackknifed up off the bed. Her hair fell into her eyes, obscuring her vision. The velvety-smooth sound of his chuckle slipped down her spine, sending tingles of awareness with it.

Her internal muscles contracted with remembered pleasure and the need for more. Willow ignored their demand.

Pushing her hair out of her face, she realized two things at once. First, the sheet was puddled in her lap leaving her bare from the waist up.

Snatching at the edge, she pulled it up to her chin.

His sinfully sculpted mouth twitched and the dark slash of a single eyebrow rose. "Little late for that, isn't it?"

Ignoring him, Willow gathered the sheet around her like a shield. It was about the only one she had left.

Pushing away from the door frame he'd negligently propped himself against, he moved into her private space with a powerful grace that made her want to hate him. His black pants were slung low on his hips, leaving the top slashes of the V of sculpted muscle visible.

She remembered running her tongue down those matching creases straight to the Promised Land they pointed to. Her skin flushed hotter.

He sank to the bed beside her, his hip dipping the mattress so she had to brace to keep from rolling against him.

Silently, he held out a mug to her. Steam curled up from the surface, bringing with it the delectable scent of coffee.

Willow narrowed her eyes, staring at it for several seconds before deciding she was really going to need the jolt.

Because the second thing she realized was that she knew exactly who had slept in her bed last night. She didn't like him. And he'd lied to her.

She fortified herself with several sips before stretching to the opposite side of the bed and setting the mug down. Better not to have this conversation with hot liquid in her hands. He might just end up burned.

He watched her, warily. Obviously he was fully prepared for the conversation they were about to have. Just one more reason to be pissed. Had he known who she was from the first moment?

Shifting away from him, Willow glared. "Your name isn't Dev."

His mouth tightened, but that was his only reaction to the accusation in her voice. "Yes, it is."

"No, it isn't."

"Interesting. That's what my birth certificate says."

"That's not funny, Wick."

"Do you see me laughing, Willow? And don't call me that."

No, he wasn't laughing. At least not on the outside. She couldn't help but think he was probably hooting and hollering on the inside about the coup he'd just pulled.

As if ruining her sister's marriage and betraying her hadn't been enough for him, he'd decided to weasel his way into getting what he'd always wanted—her, naked.

Although, she had to admit, she'd been pretty eager to shed her clothes last night and hadn't put up much of a fuss.

Guilt and regret mixed with her anger, blunting it in a way that was far from satisfying. Trust her conscience to surface just when she needed righteous indignation.

She'd had a one-night stand with a stranger. A masked stranger. She hadn't exactly expected to wake up with a paragon of virtue. But she hadn't expected to wake up with Wick, either. The only man who'd ever tempted her to sin.

A groan rolled up through her chest, but she cut it off before it broke free. That alone should have told her who touched her. No one had ever made her feel so electrified and alive with nothing more than a look.

He'd always had that effect on her. But she hadn't seen him in ten years and had no reason to expect him in Sweetheart—let alone beneath the devil's mask.

"Why not? What's wrong with Wick?"

"It isn't my name. Never has been. The only people who've ever called me that are the people in this town. And, as you can imagine, I don't like the reminder very much."

They'd called him Wicked Wick. She remembered hearing her sister purr his name, the single word filled with the kind of raw sensuality that, at seventeen, she hadn't completely understood.

Oh, she did now. An unwanted shiver of memory erupted in goose bumps across her skin.

To hide her reaction, Willow climbed from the bed, making sure the sheet stayed tightly wrapped around her body. With the bed between them she felt a little steadier. Until those midnight eyes full of banked heat and promise raked across her.

"Why are you here?"

Standing, Dev rounded the bed, never breaking his hold on her gaze. She grudgingly gave him credit. After that one brief singeing glance, he kept his focus squarely on her face.

He closed the space between them. Willow shifted, trying to get far enough away that she could think clearly. And deal with the situation. But there was nowhere for her to go.

Her back hit the edge of the dresser. Behind her, several bottles and trinkets trembled at the contact. Straightening her spine, Willow pulled the shreds of her composure around her like a shield. She refused to let him see that he got to her.

But he didn't stop. His body crowded into her space. Her back bowed under the pressure of his presence. The heat of him overwhelmed her. He didn't touch her, but he didn't have to.

The wide expanse of his naked chest spread out before her. She couldn't swallow. She wanted to touch, but somehow found the force of will to clench her fists tighter into the sheet instead.

Even in the light of day, the dark, wicked edge that made him irresistible was there. She fully understood why every girl within a certain age range—and several outside of it—had thrown themselves at Wick…Dev… when he'd lived in Sweetheart.

Not even she had been immune to the draw of him. She'd hardly been worldly, but that kind of tense beauty was hard to miss. He'd always exuded a sensuality that just begged to be tamed.

Apparently the pull had only gotten stronger. At least, on her.

The flat of his palms pressed against the mirror behind her. She reacted to him, every cell coming alive with remembered pleasure and hopeful anticipation.

Traitor.

This man had ruined her sister's life. And if she wasn't careful he'd hurt her, as well. Again.

Dark blue eyes bored into hers. She couldn't read his expression. Gone was the sensual, giving man of last night. He'd been replaced by someone harder and more perilous.

Whatever he called himself now, he had no moral compass. Because if he did, he would have told her last night exactly who he was. Not given her a name she wouldn't recognize.

"Why am I here?" His voice was soft and dangerous. A prickle of unease shot down her spine. "In your bedroom or in town?"

"Either. Both. Ten years is a long time. Why are you back now?"

"I'm in town because I'm the landscape designer for the new resort."

Willow pulled in a shallow gasp. A devilish grin played across his lips, but it didn't quite fully form. He was holding back. And enjoying her shocked reaction.

Bastard.

What kind of game was he playing? And why was he

using her? Had last night been some kind of sick pay-back for what had happened between them?

God, she hoped not. But she was afraid she'd played right into his hands.

He lifted a lock of her hair, running it through his thumb and finger from crown to tip. The back of his hand brushed against the side of her breast. Willow sucked in a breath. His eyes sharpened. And her body burst into life.

His voice was a caress all its own, low and sultry. She couldn't help remembering the sinful words he'd whispered to her last night. "I'm in your bedroom be-cause you asked me to take you to bed."

God, she wanted him. Still. Even knowing what he'd done and how he'd deceived her last night, her body craved his touch.

Somehow she found the strength to say, "You should leave." But the words trembled. She hoped he didn't hear the waver.

Something sharp flared deep in his eyes. His mouth tightened and beside her head the fingers pressed hard to the mirror flexed dangerously. His eyelids slid down, hiding the rest of his reaction from her.

He smoldered with anger. This close to him, she could practically smell the brimstone and fire of it. But he didn't move. Instead, he let his hot eyes travel across her face for several seconds.

Willow couldn't breathe. She waited.

"We aren't done, Willow."

"Oh, yes we are. You ruined my sister's life, Wick. Dev. Whoever the hell you are."

His head recoiled as if she'd hit him. Bringing them

nose to nose, he stared into her, straight down to her soul. "You know exactly who I am, angel."

"Last night was a mistake. If I'd known who you were it never would have happened."

"I know."

Everything inside her stilled. Those two words managed to cut through the fog of desire he was weaving around her.

"What do you mean, you know? Exactly when did you figure out who I was?"

"The moment I got my hands on you. And once I touched you, I knew I couldn't let you go until I'd had more."

"So to hell with what I might have wanted?"

"Don't kid yourself, angel. We both know you got exactly what you wanted last night. A taste of the wild side with a depraved devil. I did the right thing and kept my hands off you once before. I wasn't about to make that same mistake twice." He pushed away from her.

She felt the loss of his warmth and hated herself a little bit for the weakness.

"You really are a bastard, aren't you?"

His mouth twisted. "Actually, no, I'm not. This town just has the ability to pull the worst out of me. Believe it or not, Willow, I had no intention of seducing you last night. I was just as overwhelmed by the friction between us as you were."

His unexpected and candid confession left her speechless. The words deflated some of the self-righteous anger she'd been using to combat her own guilt and embarrassment.

He'd even taken that.

But before she could say anything more, he snatched the rest of his clothes from the chair in the corner and walked out.

Although not before getting in one last parting shot. "You're old enough to know better than to believe everything you hear, Willow. You have no idea what happened between Rose and me. But I promise you, it was nothing like last night."

WILLOW TRIED TO go on with her day, to pretend nothing had happened, but it was difficult. In a bid for distraction, she barricaded herself in her design studio and tried to lose herself in the dress she was making for a country music star who had recently crossed over and become a pop sensation. She was also marrying one of the most well-known quarterbacks in the NFL.

Unfortunately, every time Willow's fingers slipped across the sumptuous silk of the dress her mind immediately jumped to the feel of Dev's skin beneath her sensitive fingertips, and her entire body would clench and burn.

Needless to say, after five hours she'd gotten very little work done while her frustration level had increased to critical mass.

Sundays were usually her most productive design days since she had the place to herself, but not today. Not even cranking up the music could drown out the distractions, not when they were coming from inside her own head. Which was just one more accusation she could lay at Dev's feet. He was costing her a day's worth of work that she couldn't afford to lose.

Willow was staring with frustration at the yards of

white clinging to the dress form when the notes of "Hell on Heels" blasted into the room. She still jumped at the unexpected interruption. Everyone in her life knew she holed up in the studio on Sundays and usually left her alone to work.

She knew from the song that it was one of her friends. Snatching up the phone she'd thrown onto the table behind her, she registered the name on the screen even as she answered.

"Hope, what's wrong?" There were only a few reasons Hope would be bothering her and none of them were good.

"What were you thinking, Willow?"

"Huh?" She was immediately lost. "What are you talking about?"

A loud sigh echoed down the line followed by a soft swear word that did nothing to settle Willow's suddenly frantic heartbeat.

Instead of answering her question, Hope said, "I'll be there in five minutes. Don't leave."

A protest was halfway out of Willow's mouth but it didn't matter. Hope had hung up, the harsh buzz of the broken line echoing through Willow's head.

She didn't have to wait long. A knock on her studio door boomed through the eerily quiet space. But it wasn't Hope who waited on the other side when she swung open the door. It was Tatum.

"Oh, shit. This must be really bad if she called in reinforcements. What is going on?"

Willow hadn't realized Tatum was carrying a laptop tucked under her arm until she brushed past and set the thing on the nearest table, popping it open. The screen blinked to life, and Willow's legs wobbled for a few seconds before she stiffened them.

Her eyes devoured the words that accompanied the photographs she couldn't seem to tear herself away from.

Dev, half-dressed, his amazingly ripped chest clearly on display, was leaving her house right around dawn. His dark eyes were furious and his harsh mouth slanted in a dangerous frown.

A shiver—that had nothing to do with the tingle of awareness and excitement—snaked down her spine. Who would take pictures of Dev leaving her house at dawn? Why? And why the heck post them online?

"Well" was all she could say, her mind whirling with too many thoughts to process any of them.

Tatum grasped her arm and pushed her into a nearby chair.

Her eyes raced over the text one more time. The gist was that the devil had returned to Sweetheart and immediately sullied the first angel he encountered.

While no one—well, no one other than Hope and Macey—knew what had happened between her and Dev ten years ago, everyone knew that he'd seduced her sister and broken up a marriage.

She groaned, closing her eyes as embarrassment flooded through her. Was it asking too much to hope that no one else had seen this?

"I don't understand the significance of what's going on, but Hope was adamant that you needed to see this immediately. The blog was posted anonymously and an email sent from a generic account to just about the entire town. And from your reaction, she was right. I'm guessing those regrets we talked about last night go a little deeper than even I anticipated. Tell me."

Willow's mouth twisted into a dangerous frown as she looked between her friend and the email that declared her sin for public consumption.

"I know him."

"God, I hope so. That man was made for sex. If he left before you got to know him that would be a crying shame."

Willow shook her head. "No, you don't understand. I already knew him before last night."

Tatum shrugged. "So?"

"He's the man who slept with my sister and ruined her marriage."

Tatum's eyes widened into large pools of shock. "Oh." Though she'd only been in Sweetheart a few years, even Tatum had heard the story about Rose and Wick. It was the kind of gossip that circulated as a cautionary tale about what not to do in Sweetheart.

"It gets better. Only a few people know this, but... he and I..."

Tatum's eyes widened. "The bastard gets around."

Heat flooded Willow's pale skin. "No. We didn't. But it was close. Rose brought him around several times. I was seventeen. He was twenty. We danced around each other for a few months. I tried very hard to be good, but you saw him...."

"Temptation on a cracker."

Willow nodded. She screwed her eyes closed, trying to shut out the memories. The heavy heat she'd been too young to understand or deal with. The overwhelming need. The oppressive pain of betrayal when she learned he'd slept with her sister.

"One night he came over looking for Rose, but she wasn't there. It was late and hot. I was in tiny shorts and a tank top."

Even now she could feel the pressure of the humid summer air on her skin. And when Wick had shown up on her porch, moonlight slashing across his hard jaw and sharp cheekbones, she'd felt as if her skin was tight enough to split. The only thing she'd known was that she needed relief.

And he'd given it to her...or a taste of it. Before she'd realized what he'd intended, her back was pressed against the house and his mouth was devouring hers. That kiss was like nothing she'd experienced before. It was hot and hard, and made her whole body ache.

She'd squirmed against him, wanting more. And he'd given it to her. Right there on the front porch where anyone could have seen. His hard body surrounded her. His hand had slipped beneath the high hem of her shorts, finding the slick heat that proved she wanted him even as she tried not to.

Just like the night before, the moment he'd touched her she was gone. She let him drive his fingers deep inside her. Within minutes he'd had her coming, hot and hard. The best orgasm she'd ever had until last night.

She'd slid back down into a boneless, panting mess, fully expecting him to take whatever he wanted from her. And she would have let him. But instead of opening his fly, he'd backed away, staring at her with hard, glittering eyes.

In that low, rasping voice that sent shivers down

her spine, he'd breathed, "Little girl." And then he'd just…left.

"Two days later the scandal with Rose broke. Apparently, he no longer wanted me. Why would he want someone so innocent and unschooled when he could have my worldly, uninhibited sister?"

Tatum blinked, one long, drawn out motion. "Jesus, Willow. And you still let him spend the night?"

Willow dropped her head into her hands and dug the heel of her palms into her eyes. "We kept the masks on. I didn't know until this morning."

Tatum let out a low whistle, the single sound conveying absolutely everything she'd struggled with since she'd learned just who was behind the mask—shock, anger, desire, betrayal, self-recriminations, unwanted need.

"Dev left town a few days later. I had no idea he was back until he walked into my bedroom this morning carrying a mug of coffee."

Tatum asked the logical question. "Did he know who you were?"

Willow nodded.

"That bastard."

Part of her wanted to let Tatum keep her poor opinion of Dev. It would be easy to bask in the unqualified support of her friend. But it wouldn't be fair.

"He gave me several opportunities to stop things, but I didn't. *I* was the one who insisted on the masks. He tried to take his off. He had to know the moment I saw his face that I'd recognize him. He wasn't deliberately trying to hide who he was from me…I did that all on my own. He even told me his name. We just called him something else when he lived here before."

The dark slash of Tatum's eyebrow winged up into a silent question.

"Devlin Warwick. Everyone called him Wick. Wicked Wick."

"Oh, yeah, that totally fits."

"Apparently he hates it and goes by Dev now. I didn't remember his full name until this morning."

This time the other eyebrow joined the first, Tatum studying her with a quizzical expression that made Willow fight the need to squirm.

"You're defending him an awful lot."

Willow made a harsh sound in the back of her throat. "I'm not defending him. I'm taking responsibility for my own actions and decisions. I'd like to let him take all the blame, but that wouldn't be fair. I made a decision—a bad one—and now I'll have to deal with the consequences. Everyone in town is going to know what I did."

"There are worse things."

"Sure, although at the moment I'm having trouble thinking of any."

Hope burst through the back door and skidded to a halt, half in and half out of Willow's workroom. Her quick eyes catalogued Tatum and the open computer, then scoured Willow's face for clues to what her response needed to be—alcohol, anger, indignation, a shotgun...they were all viable options, depending.

Willow saved her the trouble of guessing. "I'm fine. Angry, sure, but not at Dev."

Tatum snorted, doing a poor job at smothering the sound.

"Okay, I'm slightly angry with Dev. I'm more upset with myself. And whoever thought it appropriate to splash my business all over the internet and then announce it to the entire town."

Had the person who'd taken the pictures been lurking outside her house, waiting? Or had they chanced on a moment of opportunity?

A nasty thought blasted through Willow's brain. Had Dev set the whole thing up? Maybe he'd had someone there waiting. She shook her head, dismissing the idea almost as soon as it surfaced.

What did he have to gain by this? If he'd been out for a little humiliating revenge he'd gotten it already. Just thinking about how inappropriate and shameless she'd been with him last night...

Besides, he'd told her that he hadn't intended to seduce her, and for some reason she believed him. Or maybe she just wanted to. Either way, she couldn't see an angle.

"Who would do something like this? And why?" Hope asked, her voice ringing with an indignation that Willow appreciated. It was nice to know she could count on her friends.

"That's a great question. They must have been right in front of your house." Tatum crossed her arms beneath her breasts and narrowed her eyes to slits.

Tatum's words drew Willow's eyes back to the screen and the photographs she'd tried to ignore. Her friend was right, they'd been taken from in front of her house, but that wasn't what kept her staring.

The first couple of pictures showed Dev exiting. Willow could practically hear the reverberation from the slammed door, his stiff shoulders and thunderous expression easy to interpret.

What had her tongue licking across suddenly dry lips was the way the black dress shirt he'd been wearing at the party hung loose and open, showing the dented planes of his abs. The gray tie trailed across his shoulders. Willow wanted to reach through the screen and run her hands across his silky skin.

The next photograph had his back turned, the tip of a red horn clearly visible sticking out from the back pocket of his slacks. Even without the mask, he was clearly dangerous enough to be a devil.

More dangerous than he'd been last night.

And still, Willow couldn't look away. She knew the sinuous twist of muscles hidden beneath the disarrayed clothing. She knew what he could do with those powerful legs and talented hands. Her body hummed with the memories, begging her to forget everything and find him for a repeat performance.

In the last photograph, Dev's head was turned in profile. He stared up at the covered windows of her bedroom. The expression on his face was partially obscured, but that didn't prevent her body from reacting. She'd seen it last night when he pushed deep inside her—predatory, dangerous, promising and sensual.

Devlin Warwick wasn't finished with her yet. He'd said as much. And she wasn't exactly sure what to think about that. Her body buzzed with anticipation. Her brain screamed a warning.

"Willow!"

"What?" She jerked her eyes away from the computer screen and up to Hope and Tatum. Both of her friends stared at her expectantly. Guilt heated her skin. Willow sighed with barely checked exasperation.

"What are you going to do?"

"I'm going to ignore him."

Tatum shook her head, fighting a smile that she couldn't quite keep from tugging at the corners of her mouth. Willow appreciated the effort even if her friend failed miserably.

"Not about Dev, about the blog post."

"Oh, that."

"Yes, that."

"I don't know. What is there to do?"

Nothing. She'd witnessed enough gossip to realize that a public search for whoever had invaded her privacy would only keep the story on everyone's tongues longer. Better to ignore it and hope everyone moved on to juicier tales soon.

She definitely had no intention of giving them any more fodder.

5

DEV WAS STILL pissed that she'd kicked him out. Although it was exactly what he'd expected her to do.

It was his problem that he'd hoped she wouldn't.

He couldn't get rid of the residual buzz of anger mixed with the constant hum of need. Not even being upset with her could stop him from wanting her again.

It had always been that way for him with Willow. The moment he'd seen her, all long, tanned legs and shy, hesitant smile, his body had gone haywire.

He hadn't known what to do with his response. She was clearly off-limits—not one of the rough and outrageous girls he usually took to bed. She'd been young, and until last night he'd assumed innocent.

Although that revelation wouldn't have changed anything.

Back then, Willow had been too good for him and he'd at least been coherent enough to realize it.

Keeping his hands off her was the hardest thing he'd ever done. Aside from walking away from her…

Spinning over the past was getting him nowhere.

He hadn't come to Sweetheart for Willow or anyone else. He'd come for himself. For closure. For a bit of friendly retribution.

He needed to drag his focus back to the point of this little venture. He had his first meeting with the head of the resort consortium, Brett Newcomb, tomorrow morning. So, to keep his head from spiraling back to the lightning-quick memories of Willow's body sliding against his, he'd spent most of the day burning off energy in his grandmother's back garden. Trying to clear out the debris left over from summer was a better use of his time. Physical labor would leave his body drained and his mind too tired to think.

Around five his stomach had begun to protest his attempt to subsist on nothing but Coke and handfuls of peanut M&M's. Since there wasn't much in the house by way of food, he decided to head to the diner in town for something real. He could practically taste the burst of a greasy hamburger across his tongue.

Dev grabbed a shower, and threw on a clean pair of jeans and a flannel button-down. Tossing the keys in his hand once and snatching them out of the air, he cranked the truck and enjoyed the rumble of the powerful engine.

He slid into a parking spot outside the diner. It was busier than he'd expected at six on a Sunday evening. Walking through the front door, he enjoyed the warmth and scent of fried food that greeted him.

Until he realized that every person in the place had turned to stare at him. And not with curiosity, but with hard-eyed anger. He'd only been in town a day, what could he have done already?

The memory of pale blue eyes, glazed with the pleasure of release flashed across his mind. A blast of cold that had nothing to do with the dropping temperatures outside shot up his spine and made the hairs on the back of his neck stand on end. She hadn't wasted time in telling everyone all about his transgressions.

Dev's first instinct was to turn around and leave, but he would not give them what they wanted. He wasn't going to let these people force him out of anywhere, least of all a damn diner. As much as they might want to, they couldn't control where he ate.

Clenching his hands into fists, Dev let a lazy scowl sweep above the crowd, ignoring everyone. He spotted an empty table wedged into the back of the room and headed for it. He contemplated putting his back to the room and everyone in it, but his spine tightened at the idea of leaving himself open and vulnerable. Instead, he settled with his back to the wall.

Slowly, everyone returned to their own conversations and dinners. The waitress came over and he placed his order.

Eating alone had never bothered him before. Not even when surrounded by other people. Tonight, it was oppressively obvious that he wasn't just alone, but being purposely ignored. Greetings rose above the din as patrons floated in and out. People leaned across the spaces between tables joining together in conversations he had no part in. Kids darted around, laughing and snatching French fries.

It bothered him, although he knew it shouldn't. These people could think whatever they wanted about him. They were wrong. And that was their problem, not his.

He munched on his burger and contemplated calling his project manager on the Cascade Properties job to check in on their progress when the bell above the door chimed again. A swirl of cool air shot through the diner, sending chilly fingers across his skin and bringing with it a scent he would never forget—honeysuckle, sandalwood and something altogether innocent. A scent that only belonged to one woman.

Looking up from his phone, Dev found Willow standing in the doorway, her gaze trained completely on him. Everyone had fallen silent again. They stared, but this time it was in Willow's direction, and instead of barely suppressed anger they were full of pity.

That bothered Dev, but he had no idea why.

Heat flamed up Willow's face, touching her cheeks. Instead of ducking to hide the reaction, her jaw tightened. Her eyes glittered with determination and challenge. Her lips pulled into a forced smile that she spread around liberally.

After a few tense moments, she began to weave through the tables, heading straight for him. Without asking, she pulled out the chair opposite him and slipped gracefully into it.

A shocked murmur rippled through the crowd. Every single eye was trained on them. Guests had come for dinner, but apparently were thrilled with the idea of getting a free show out of the deal, as well.

While everyone else watched them, Dev watched *her.* And waited. Whatever Willow wanted, the grim expression on her face told him he wasn't going to enjoy it.

"I'm sorry."

Those were not the words he'd expected to fall from her lush, pink, enchantingly kissable lips.

Tilting his head to the side, Dev considered her for several moments. Was she apologizing for kicking him out? For her anger? For believing the worst of him? There were so many options. "For what?"

"For the blog."

Okay, now he was confused. Not only did he have no idea what she was talking about, but it wasn't even on his list. Why would he care what some bored housewife posted on the internet? What could that possibly have to do with him?

"You don't know." Willow's flat voice sent a tingle that tightened his scalp with apprehension.

Her face screwed up and she squinched her eyes closed for several seconds. Blowing out a long, slow breath, she opened them again.

"Someone posted pictures of you leaving my house this morning online and then emailed the link to a huge list of people."

He blinked, trying to figure out what the problem was. Who cared?

"You were half naked."

Heat crept up Willow's pale skin. Oh, she cared.

The anger he'd been fighting all day slammed back through his body, turning his muscles rigid. Leaning across the table, he ground out, "Are you more embarrassed that you slept with me or that the whole town knows about it?"

Her eyes widened. A jumble of emotions chased across her pale blue eyes—shock, hurt, chagrin and finally fury. Her eyes glittered like broken glass, cutting through him just as easily.

He regretted the words almost as soon as they'd left his mouth. What was it about this woman that drove him to the brink and then shoved him straight off the cliff of decent behavior?

But he refused to take the words back. There might have been a better way to couch the question, but it was still valid. What bothered her more? That she'd broken her own rules and let him in or that everyone now had proof that she wasn't as perfect as she liked to pretend?

Her body tightened, her hands flattening on the table as she prepared to stand up. "This was a mistake. I shouldn't have bothered to come tell you."

Before she could move, Dev's hand shot across the table. His fingers wrapped around her wrist, holding on and anchoring her in place.

Her gasp was soft enough that it was almost drowned out by the clatter around them, but he heard it. And watched as her pupils dilated and her jaw set against the reaction she didn't want, but couldn't control any more than he apparently could.

"Why did you?"

"Because I thought you should know. I have no idea who posted the pictures, but it wasn't because they were being nice. I'm hoping it was nothing more than a cruel joke, but who knows?"

"You think this is about me."

She took a deep breath. The motion of her breasts, pushing tight against the soft shirt that clung to her skin, made his mouth go dry with the need to taste her again.

"You're the only one in the pictures. They appear the

day after you arrive back in town. It isn't a great leap to the idea that whatever this is, it's about you."

She was worried about him. The realization slammed into him so hard that he let her go and rocked back into his chair. Her palm, still flat on the table, flexed as if she'd just escaped from a tight, uncomfortable binding.

It had been a long time since anyone had been concerned for him.

A warm buzz started somewhere in the center of his chest and spread slowly through the rest of him.

"I appreciate your concern, but it's unnecessary."

"Who said I was concerned?"

He snagged her gaze, holding her in place and refusing to let her go. His lips tugged up into a lopsided grin that dared her to lie to him again.

She didn't bother. "Just be careful. You weren't exactly considered citizen of the year before. I don't want what happened between us to derail your job with the resort."

"Well, that's sweet, angel, but my contract with the consortium is airtight. The only way the citizens of Sweetheart are getting rid of me this time is if I don't perform. And we both know I have no problems in that department."

Dev enjoyed the way her cheeks flamed with color. Her eyes flashed a warning. His body hummed, this verbal sparring with her doing nothing to quench the flame of need licking across his skin. In fact, it only made him want her more.

Ten years ago she'd been quiet and unsure. Delicate. She still had that edge of fragility that made a man want to circle around her and growl at anything that came within inches of touching her. But she no longer held back, unafraid to call him on his bullshit and slap him across the face with her harsh words.

Willow Portis had grown up, and God, that only made him want her more. She'd been a tempting teenager. She was a formidable woman.

She'd pulled her long, sleek hair into a smooth knot at the back of her head—now the deep, dark brown that he remembered. He wanted to tug on it and make the silky strands tumble down across his hands and chest and thighs. He wanted to run his teeth along the elegant curve of her long neck. He wanted to leave a mark on her so that every time she looked at it her body would remember.

Instead, he clenched his hands tight in his lap beneath the table and dragged a heavy breath into his burning lungs.

He needed to put some distance between them. Now. Before he did something stupid and compounded the problems they already had.

"Look, I appreciate the thought, but you don't need to worry about me. I've been taking care of myself for most of my life." By force of will, Dev tore his eyes from hers. The moment his attention drifted over the crowd of people around them, guilty stares started jerking away.

Nothing ever changed.

His lips twisted into a scowl and he said, "You better leave now. A few more minutes sitting here with me and your reputation will be ruined forever."

Dismissing her, he dipped several fries into the pile of ketchup on his plate and shoved them into his mouth.

But she didn't leave. Instead, she shifted on her chair, as if she were finding a softer spot to settle. Willow Portis was a disconcerting puzzle. Just when he thought he'd pegged her, she went and did something that broke the neat box he'd shoved her into.

Watching him through lowered lids, she crossed her arms over her chest and glared back at him.

"You really are an asshole, aren't you?"

Her words hurt, although he didn't want them to. And he certainly wasn't going to let her know it. Swirling another fry through the pool of red, he said lazily, "Yep, that's me."

"What did Rose ever see in you?"

He sent her a mischievous grin, the sexual energy he was trying to keep a tight lid on leaking out.

"Rose got exactly what she wanted from me."

Willow huffed deep in the back of her throat.

"I seriously doubt that. She had to leave town. You both did. Nothing is worth losing your home, especially not sex."

"Speak for yourself, little girl. Finally getting a taste of you was worth a whole hell of a lot."

She gasped, enraged. God, he'd always enjoyed watching her shoulders tighten with indignation and her eyes narrow with determination. Ten years ago it was the only kind of passion he'd let himself have from her. Except that one night…

What bothered him most about the conversation was the obvious role Willow had cast Rose in—the victim. The little vixen had been far from innocent.

"Rose left town because she wanted to, Willow."

Willow shook her head. "Rose left because she didn't have a choice."

Dev swore, long and low. Luckily, he was smart enough to keep the worst of his response inside his own head. "She had plenty of choices. She did exactly what she wanted. She always did."

Even he could hear the bitter edge to his words, but apparently Willow was too caught up in her indignation to notice.

"Is that what you tell your guilty conscience? Rose is a showgirl in Vegas, Dev. She dances topless. Because she couldn't do anything else to earn money when her husband divorced her."

How had Willow's vision of her sister become so skewed?

"And she loves every minute of it. She's the center of attention. Men fawn over her. They desire her. No doubt she has a string of them that she's taking for everything they're worth. Don't kid yourself. We both know your sister can take care of herself just fine. She's manipulative and ruthlessly beautiful…and she knows it."

Willow's eyes flashed a warning, but he had no intention of heeding it. Rose had cost him plenty and he wasn't going to pull any punches, not even for her sister.

The legs of her chair scraped loudly against the floor. Willow stood. She glared down at him, her body tight with contemptuous disdain. It should bother him. On anyone else it probably would have. But with Willow… the haughty expression just made him want to ruffle her pristine feathers again. To drag her down into the muck with him and show her just how much fun it could be to get dirty.

To make her remember—and admit—how satisfying last night had been. And that she wanted desperately to do it again. Just as badly as he did.

"I refuse to listen to you malign my sister." When she left the diner, her palms slapped the front door with a resounding smack. A whirling gust of wind blasted in, fluttering the papers tacked to the bulletin board by the door.

Throwing a twenty down onto the table, Dev followed her.

This conversation wasn't over.

6

WILLOW SEETHED. How dare he talk about Rose that way? He was the reason she'd gotten into trouble in the first place. If he'd kept his tempting smile and those challengingly sensual eyes to himself then her sister never would have made the mistakes that she had.

And Willow wouldn't have been left feeling betrayed by them both. Although she really didn't want to think about that. Ten years was a long time and she'd moved on. Let it go. Everyone had their heart broken as a teenager…it was a rite of passage. Dev had been hers.

There was no reason to compound the stupidity by letting him get to her again. She was older and smarter now. And she saw beneath the crap he was pedaling.

But maybe that was the problem. He'd said exactly what she'd expected him to—poked and prodded at her just as he'd always done—but unlike before, something told her there was more to his barbed comments.

Was he just giving her what she expected?

Rose had been wild long before Dev had come into her life. Her sister had delighted in ignoring the rules. If her parents set a curfew, Rose broke it. If they told her not to wear something, she hid the clothes and changed the moment she was out of their sight. If they told her not to date someone, she spent hours outside in the driveway necking with him.

About the only thing she'd done that her parents had approved of was marrying Marcus. He was older, and comfortable enough to take care of her. Rose wasn't a good student and college had definitely not been in her future.

And Rose had enjoyed being treated like a princess. Her husband had showered her with jewelry and trips and a brand-new car. For a twenty-year-old the easy lifestyle had been seductive, and only two months after meeting him Rose had eloped.

Willow's mind spun back to the past, one she tried hard to forget. Things had seemed fine for a few months. Rose settled down a bit. She spent her time getting her nails done and going shopping. She was happy.

And then it all exploded. Rose began staying out all night again. She got into trouble, even calling late one night so that their parents could bail her out of jail. Several times her husband showed up at their house in the middle of the night looking for her. Willow remembered the loud, angry voices.

She'd tried to talk to Rose, but her sister had been tight-lipped, telling her everything would be fine.

And then the rumors about her and Wick had started...just days after he'd walked away from her. She'd confronted Rose. With dreamy eyes, her sister had said Wick was her ticket out of Sweetheart. And Willow had been devastated.

But she shouldn't have been. She knew his reputation, a scandalous loner who never stayed with anyone for very long. They'd never even dated. Aside from that one night on her porch, he'd never touched her.

She'd felt like an idiot, but couldn't stop it from hurting.

He hadn't even stood by Rose. Within days of the scandal breaking, Wick was gone.

And that pissed her off more than anything. He'd been playing with Willow. She accepted that. But he'd destroyed Rose's life and then walked away as if it was no big deal.

Willow's heels slapped against the pavement as she walked down Main toward her store. It was dark already, and she wished she'd grabbed her coat before slipping down the street. When she'd locked up the studio and noticed Dev's truck sitting in the diner's lot she knew she needed to talk to him.

She was only half a block from the diner when Levi Waite materialized on the sidewalk beside her. Before she knew what was happening, her back was pressed against the crumbling brick and his hands were lodged on either side of her body. He leaned into her personal space, although he didn't actually touch her, at least not after he'd caught her by surprise and spun her around.

"Now, Willow, if you'd wanted company last night why didn't you just call me? I'm a much better choice than Warwick. I wouldn't have been sneaking out of your house before dawn. If you'd taken me home we'd still be locked up tight inside your bedroom."

That first kick of surprise sent a burst of adrenaline through Willow's blood, but her brain quickly realized there wasn't a threat and cut off the reaction. Levi Waite was harmless, if rather annoying.

She reached up to elbow him away, but before her sharp elbow could connect with his soft belly the man was flying backward. It was as if an invisible string had been tied to his waist. His body folded in half, arms and legs flailing as he lost his balance and found himself ass-down in a heap on the pavement.

"Keep your hands off the lady," Dev growled, staring down at Levi with enough barely checked heat to keep Sweetheart warm through winter.

Levi wasn't smart enough to realize he was outclassed by Dev, who was bigger and carried more muscle. Or maybe he did and his pride wouldn't let him stay down. Either way, he reacted on instinct, scrambling up from the ground and lunging for the man who'd knocked him silly without warning.

With a sigh, Willow stepped between the two men. With a hand to Levi's chest, she said, "Stop."

Dev grasped her by the waist and tried to pull her out from the middle of the testosterone sandwich. But that wasn't going to work for her. She dug her heels in and grounded her weight. Tossing a glare at Dev over her shoulder, she warned, "Back off."

Something in his eyes warned her he wasn't going to listen.

Instead, she turned her attention to someone with the potential for a level head.

Looking Levi in the eye, she said, "Get out of here. And if you ever grab me like that again I'm going to knee your nuts up into your throat first and ask questions later. Understand?"

Levi met Willow's glare and sized up Dev straining behind her. Apparently deciding that leaving held merit, he nodded and slipped away.

Willow waited until he was safely inside the diner before she turned on Dev.

"What were you thinking?"

"That you were in trouble and someone needed to help you."

A sound of frustration buzzed through Willow's chest. God save her from men.

"I didn't need any help. I was handling it."

The urge to wipe the skeptical expression off his face was strong, but somehow she found the strength to deny it. Just.

"Please, little girl, you're barely strong enough to swat a fly, let alone knock some sense into that Neanderthal."

Little girl. God, she hated when he called her that. It had always made her feel awkward and out of her element...although everything about Wick had made her feel out of her element. She might have deserved the nickname he'd delighted in throwing in her face then, but now...

Her teeth ground together beneath the weight of her anger. Her elbow flashed out. "I'm no little girl. Not anymore."

Unfortunately, she didn't find a target. The damn man was fast. Before she realized what was happening the world was spinning. Shadows surrounded them, blocking out the streetlights and weak moonlight. Her back collided with something solid and her wrists were pinned above her.

Willow blinked, trying to get her bearings. They were in the alley. Her mouth opened, air whistling past dry lips as she pulled oxygen into her lungs.

A block away were people and lights. Laughter and conversation. But here, in the dark with Dev, it felt as if they were utterly alone. Separate from everyone and everything. She thought maybe she should feel afraid, but she didn't. Instead, an unwanted thrill raced across her skin.

"Trust me, I'm fully aware that you're all woman." Dev's voice was silky, smooth and deadly. Her body reacted, pulsing to life at nothing more than the appreciation in his tone.

How could he make her feel this way with nothing more than a few well-chosen words? Wanted. Excited. Alive.

It had been a long time since anyone had made her feel that way.

Why did Devlin Warwick have to be the man to set her on fire? If any other guy made her burn the way Dev did, she'd give in and enjoy whatever he had in mind.

But Dev was the man holding her wrists above her head. She flexed her hands, testing whether or not he was satisfied with the point he was trying to make. But he didn't let her go. Instead, the band of his fingers tightened a little more.

A wicked glint flashed through his midnight eyes. The only place he touched her was her wrists, but that didn't seem to matter. She could *feel* him. The heat. The intent. A pulsing need that snapped between them, electricity just waiting for the circuit to close and shock them both.

"How are you going to get out of this one, angel?" His voice drawled with lazy curiosity, but something told her it was all an act. She didn't have to touch him to know his muscles were taut with anticipation.

And all she had to do was look down to know that he was just as turned on as she was. Not even the dark shadows could hide the major hard-on straining against the fly of his jeans. They looked soft and worn, as though, with the right pressure, the material might just rip open and show her everything hidden beneath.

Unconsciously, Willow's tongue darted out to pass across her dry lips.

He groaned. His eyelids slid down but couldn't quite hide the glitter of need behind them.

She was doing that to him. He wanted her. The baddest bad boy she'd ever met, the legendary lover who'd rocked her world and given her the best orgasm of her life, was standing in front of her, hard and throbbing because he wanted to touch her. Touch. *Her.*

The realization was heady. Without thought, a challenge she'd had no intention of issuing fell from her lips, "Maybe I don't want out of anything."

Shit. She was going to regret that statement.

"Jesus, Willow, are you trying to kill me?"

But probably not yet.

In a surge, he was against her. She was caught between the unyielding wall and the hard press of his body. His mouth found the column of her throat, latching on and sucking hard.

Her knees buckled; the only thing keeping her upright was his hold on her wrists.

"I've wanted to do that all night. Do you know how good you taste?"

She couldn't make her throat work so she shook her head instead. Really, she'd never thought about it. Foreplay was something to get you from point A to point B. With Dev, it felt like a whole hell of a lot more.

Every nerve ending in her body was lit up like the town Christmas tree.

His mouth found hers and she sighed. With nothing more than the insistent pressure of his lips, he tugged her down into the maelstrom of desire he was building around her. His tongue stroked deep, invading and teasing, making her internal muscles clamp tight between her thighs.

He pulled away and stared down at her. They were centimeters apart, she'd been blessedly naked for him just last night, but she couldn't fight the feeling that in this moment she was so much more vulnerable. That he could see more than she wanted him to.

"One taste of you is not enough. Do you know how hard it was for me to walk away from you?"

"I didn't give you much choice." Her voice trembled, evidence of the fine tremor that had taken up residence in her muscles.

He shook his head. "I don't mean last night. Ten years ago I had you just like this. Up against a wall in the dark. Alone."

Every muscle in her body stiffened. For the first time since he'd taken possession of her wrists, she struggled against his hold.

"Oh, no, you don't," he growled.

"If you wanted to keep me interested then you probably shouldn't have brought up the night you left me panting on my front porch to go screw my sister."

His head snapped back as if she'd slapped him. "What?"

"That night. You left me and went to Rose. You found a girl who knew exactly what she was doing, not a child who couldn't even kiss correctly."

A harsh breath whistled through his teeth. His jaw went stone-hard and his eyes were flinty chips. He was pissed. Well, so was she.

But instead of arguing with her, he leaned forward and pressed his forehead to hers. His eyes slid shut, cutting off her window into what he was thinking. Tiny lines at the corners of his eyes flared out and the edge of his lips pulled down.

When he opened his eyes again Willow was surprised to see the anger gone, replaced by a bone-deep regret that made her breath back into her lungs.

"I didn't walk away because I didn't want you. I walked away because I wanted you too much. I thought you were a virgin, Willow. I didn't want to take you against the side of the damn house. And I didn't want you to make a hasty decision that you'd regret."

Wait. What?

"I went home and jacked off to the thought of getting you naked. Twice. And even that wasn't enough. I still woke up the next morning with a monster hard-on that wouldn't go away."

His body slid against hers, fracturing the thoughts that were racing around inside her head.

"This is what I wanted to do with you and wouldn't let myself."

His mouth found the open V of her shirt and skimmed across the edge of her collarbone. He popped the first several buttons until he found the lacy edge of her bra and slipped inside. Even before he touched her, her nipples were tight, aching points.

Letting go, the hand that had been holding her skimmed down the exposed underside of her arm. Her elbows collapsed, her hands landing heavily on his shoulders. Her muscles tingled as the blood rushed back into them. She hadn't even realized they'd gone numb.

Before she realized what he was going to do, Dev's body collapsed in front of her, his knees hitting the hard ground.

"Wait…don't…" she tried to protest, but the words wouldn't quite form.

Looking up at her through heavy lids, he said, "Let me show you exactly what I wanted to do that night."

A steady throb of need centered deep in her belly. This should have bothered her, letting him touch her, expose her in a place where anyone could see them. But she couldn't find the will to stop him. Wanting the heat of his mouth on her was more important than the possibility of discovery.

And part of her wanted to know. Wanted to believe that he'd had a difficult time letting her go. That he'd wanted her as much as she'd wanted him. That he'd been just as overwhelmed…

Callused fingers slipped beneath the hem of her skirt, pushing it inch by inch up the smooth expanse of her thigh. Her breathing was loud in her own ears, mixing with the silence of the night.

Willow watched him, unable to tear her eyes away.

He leaned forward and ran his stubble-covered jaw across the skin he was exposing. A quiver shot through her and goose bumps chased across her skin.

And he watched her, his eyes never leaving hers. That single-minded concentration made her want to squirm.

The roughened pads of his fingers slipped around the bottom of her hip to cup her rear and he groaned. "There's my fallen angel," he whispered as he realized nothing covered her cheeks. He kept going until he found the tiny string that ran along the dent there. "You really do have a naughty streak."

"I like sexy underwear. There's nothing wrong with that."

"Do you hear me complaining? I'm just upset that I can't rip this skirt off so I can get the full effect."

A thrill shot through her, but she clamped down on it, shaking her head instead.

He laughed, the grating sound heavy with suppressed longing. "How about a compromise?"

"What did you have in mind?"

Hooking his fingers in the waistband, he tugged the small bit of black lace over her hips and legs. Silently, he asked her to step out, and she did. With an appreciative smile on his lips, he tucked her panties into his back pocket.

"I'll just keep them, instead."

Oh, holy…the idea of him walking around with her panties in his pocket should have freaked her out. Instead, she found it entirely erotic.

"But I like those. They match my bra."

"So now whenever you wear it you'll think of me and what I'm about to do to you."

He didn't wait for her response, but swooped in and took what he wanted. His tongue slid over her sex, lapping at her as if she were the best thing he'd ever tasted.

She sagged against the wall, letting it take all of her weight. Her legs trembled, but her hips bumped forward, searching for so much more.

His fingers were already slippery with the evidence of her desire as he spread her open. The soft, cool breeze brushed against her sensitized skin. And then the heat of his mouth was there instead.

He found her clit and stroked it, the talented tip of his tongue driving her insane.

Hands buried deep in his hair, she hung on, searching for a safety line in the storm of sensation that was invading her.

He nipped. He sucked. He drove her to the edge and then backed off again, leaving her a whimpering mass of need.

"Please, Dev," she finally managed to whisper, unsure she could take one more moment of the delicious tension without falling apart.

One, two, three more flicks and she was flying. She tried to muffle her cry, but wasn't sure she succeeded. Wasn't sure she really cared. Waves of pleasure washed over her, taking the tension away and leaving her languid.

If she'd had trouble standing before, now the only thing keeping her from collapsing into a pile on the ground was Dev's strong hands around her waist.

He rose in a smooth, controlled motion. His hands

slipped up her body to cup the back of her neck. He angled her up to him, claiming her mouth in a possessive kiss that had her tingling all over again.

She tasted herself on his tongue, that realization more intimate than anything he'd just done to her. And she liked it.

Her brain returned by degrees. Finally, she was coherent enough to say, "Well, hell, now I'm really pissed you walked away. Although maybe it was better. I would have spent the past ten years trying to chase another orgasm like that and something tells me it'd be hard to find."

A surprised chuckle blasted from him, tickling across her temple and stirring the hair that had fallen from the knot.

His arms tightened around her. The heavy press of his erection jutted against her belly and the embers of the flames he'd just extinguished stirred to life again. She squirmed. He hissed out a choked breath. And she started to reach for him, but a sound startled them both.

A metallic rattle sounded from the opening of the alley. Dev's gaze jerked in that direction. Willow tried to jump away from him, but his tight hold on her wouldn't let her move.

He shifted his body, tucking her behind him so that he was between her and whatever was at the other end of the alley.

"Stay here," he ordered. Before she could protest, he was striding away. Willow frowned and waited only a couple of beats before following him. Egotistical man.

His sharp glare was traveling up and down the empty street when she reached him.

He threw an exasperated glare at her over his shoulder. "I thought I told you to stay put."

"Just because you can make me come doesn't mean you get to tell me what to do, hotshot."

Shaking his head, he said, "I don't see anything. Maybe it was a cat or something."

She shrugged. "Possibly." There weren't a lot of stray animals in Sweetheart, especially around Main Street. It was the heart of the tiny town and everyone worked hard to keep it clean and inviting. But it wasn't as if there was a better explanation.

Grabbing her hand, Dev hauled her up next to him and tucked her beneath his arm. "I'll walk you to your car."

He was propelling her down the street before she could protest.

"Where are your keys?"

Willow looked helplessly up at him, feeling irritated by his pushy attitude, but somehow swept up by it, as well. Like the unavoidable pull of the moon on the tide.

Fishing inside her purse, she pulled them out. Dev took them from her, unlocking her door and holding it open for her.

Leaning down, he kissed her mouth. "Good night, Willow."

"Wait." She blinked. "What about…?" Her voice trailed off. Her skin flamed hot. Her eyes tracked downward to the obvious bulge behind his fly.

His mouth quirked up into a self-deprecating, half smile. "At least this time when I dream about you I'll have reality to fill in the blanks."

The soft slide of his fingers against her cheek left her skin tingling.

"I'm not making the same mistake twice, Willow. There are obviously a few things we need to talk about before we go any further."

"Don't you think it's a little late for that?"

"No. Last night was a fantasy for you. I get that. The next time I have you in bed, I want you to know that it's me touching you. I don't want any masks or mis-understandings between us. But this isn't the kind of conversation we need to have on a dark street. It's late. You're drained. I'll wait."

Willow sucked in a sharp breath. It would have been easier if he'd let the lust overwhelm her. Taken the de-cision from her so that she could let go and think with her body instead of her brain.

But he was right. There were things they needed to talk about. And she needed to decide whether or not she could forgive him for what he'd done ten years ago.

"Dammit, I hate it when you're right," she finally said with a resigned breath.

"Angel, I'm always right," he said as she slipped into her car. Closing the door, he watched as she pulled out and drove way.

The last thing she saw was Dev standing alone on the sidewalk outside her store. Tall and forbidding. Dark and dangerous. Sexy as hell.

What was she getting herself into?

7

THE MOMENT WILLOW'S car disappeared around the corner Dev regretted letting her go—even if it had been the right thing to do. Walking away from her ten years ago had been the right thing, too, and look what that had gotten them. A big, fat mess.

He still didn't understand how she could think he'd gone from kissing her to banging her sister. He'd been a shameless prick back then, but that was a line even he wouldn't have crossed. And especially not with Willow.

Hell, he'd walked away because she was too good for him. Anything aside from going home alone that night would have just proven his point. And he'd desperately wanted something to prove him wrong.

He'd wanted to deserve her, which was why he'd gone.

Doing the right thing had never been his strong suit. He was more comfortable with breaking the rules than obeying them. Back then, he'd failed no matter what. Might as well do it in a spectacular fashion than let people think the failure was his choice.

He hadn't realized just how remarkably he'd screwed up with Willow until last night. The thought that he'd left a permanent emotional scar on her bothered him. He had plenty of his own and really wished Willow could escape without any. Although he realized that probably wasn't logical.

His persistent hard-on wasn't entirely happy with his decision, either. And, unlike before, the thought of going home and taking care of himself held absolutely no appeal. Not when he'd had a taste of the real thing.

So he tossed and turned all night, the few snatches of sleep he got filled with erotic dreams of Willow.

The next morning he was grumpy and horny, a lethal combination. Especially considering the conversation he planned to have with Willow later.

He was going to have to figure out a way to bleed off some of the tension snapping through him before they talked or all the good intentions from last night would probably go flying out the window the moment he saw her.

Which was why he was heading back out to the re-sort site. The subcontractor he'd hired to collect and run soil samples had arrived today. Brett had already called him to let him know the men were hard at work. Oversight wasn't exactly what he'd had in mind, but maybe there'd be a pile of dirt he could shovel.

If not, he'd offer to help the clearing crew and chop down a damn tree.

The soles of his steel-toed work boots had barely touched the ground when his cell phone rang. A groan escaped as he glanced at the screen. The last thing he needed was a call from his ex-wife's new high-priced lawyer. Not today.

He answered anyway, knowing he really didn't have a choice.

Three months earlier he'd gotten a frantic call from Natalie. It was the first time he'd heard from her in almost six years. And even before she'd dropped her bomb, he hadn't been excited about the prospect of catching up.

While their two-year marriage had dissolved with little drama—neither of them had cared enough to fight at that point—he still didn't relish revisiting that time in his life.

He'd been trying to find something to fill in the holes left by his mother, father and grandparents. He'd been back in college to finish his last two years and was finally starting to feel like he was on the path to normal. When Natalie had popped into his life she'd just added to the illusion.

Beautiful, graceful, funny and sweet, she'd been the kind of woman advertising campaigns told every man they wanted. Their relationship had been a bit of a whirlwind, and before he'd realized what was happening they were married. But the strain of living together quickly ended the fantasy of the fairy tale.

She'd graduated a year ahead of him and gotten a job offer in California. And she hadn't asked him to go with her when she accepted. Six months later divorce papers arrived on his doorstep, and he hadn't thought twice before signing them.

Unfortunately, he also hadn't followed up to make sure they'd been filed correctly. He'd let Natalie take care of everything, and he was paying the price for that now.

When she'd gone to apply for a new marriage license with the guy she'd been seeing for four years, they'd discovered that her half-assed lawyer hadn't processed the paperwork correctly.

She'd called Dev in a panic. She could push the divorce through without him if she wanted, but that would take time. They'd scrambled to move the wedding date. The venue was already rebooked. Her fiancé was flying her entire family in from Georgia. She'd asked for Dev's cooperation in fixing the problem.

Since he'd been just as anxious to end the marriage, they'd started the process again. New lawyer, new paperwork. Dev had signed it, popped everything into the FedEx envelope and immediately forgotten about it. And Natalie. Again.

As far as he was concerned, they hadn't been married in a very long time. Who cared what the state of Georgia said?

"Mr. Warwick, I'm so glad that I reached you," the lawyer said, reminding him that he needed to pay attention to the call. "I just wanted to let you know that everything has been filed with the courts."

"Wonderful. How long before the divorce is final?"

He made a noncommittal sound through the crackling static. Newcomb was going to have to invest in a cell tower if he wanted his guests to have reception out here in the middle of nowhere. "That's difficult to say. A few weeks, probably. This is an uncontested divorce with no complications like children or alimony. Y'all have been living apart for years so there are no assets to split. The ruling is nothing more than a formality."

No joke. At least Natalie's lawyer got it.

"Well, the sooner the better. Please let me know when you hear anything."

"Of course."

Dev ended the call and frowned down at his cell phone. Until that moment he hadn't even thought about his divorce…and whether or not he needed to tell Willow about what was going on.

Scraping a hand over his face, Dev closed his eyes. Jesus, as if things weren't complicated between them already. They had enough misunderstandings to sort through. The last thing he needed was to add one more.

She'd only been back in his life for a few days. For now he was going to keep this to himself. In a few weeks it wouldn't be an issue anyway.

"Problem?" Brett Newcomb slid up beside him, arms crossed over his wide chest. The business suit should have been out of place in the middle of the noise and construction and trees, but it wasn't. Dev had spent enough time around businessmen to recognize a guy with confidence and power. He'd learned quickly where to concentrate his efforts when selling his company's services.

"No." He shook his head, making the word stronger. "No. Just some personal stuff that won't go away."

Newcomb pursed his lips but nodded. "As long as it isn't a problem with the resort."

"Nope, not at all. So far, everything looks perfect. My team is running the samples now. We'll have the results soon. I've gotten some preliminary data on the run-off and need to sit down with you about a few adjustments I'd like to make, but they're nothing major. I think they'll actually offer us the opportunity to be more green."

"Excellent. We really want to push the environmentally friendly angle."

Dev understood and appreciated that Newcomb and the rest of the consortium were open to that. Green often meant more expensive, but usually paid for itself in the long run in decreased energy costs.

"Great. Any chance you need an extra pair of hands? I've got plenty of experience in basic construction and know how to swing a hammer and ax without maiming anyone."

Newcomb's single dark eyebrow lifted in a silent question. "Wanna tell me why you need a physical outlet?"

"Not particularly."

"Wouldn't have anything to do with Willow Portis would it?"

Dev groaned before he could stop himself. Just hearing her name made his cock jump to attention.

The bastard staring at him tried unsuccessfully to bite back a smirk.

"Putting you through hell, is she? Willow looks sweet and innocent, but underneath all the polish there's a spine of steel."

"Don't I know it."

"Lexi mentioned you guys had some sort of history."

Dev clenched his jaw. "You could say that."

"Fair warning, everyone likes Willow."

"Why wouldn't they? She'd bend over backward for anyone."

Brett jerked his head in quick agreement.

"She might not have family here in Sweetheart anymore, but she's got plenty of people who care about her. You hurt her and you'll have to deal with me...and probably Gage Harper." Brett shuddered. "Trust me, you do not want to go toe-to-toe with him. He's ex-military, protective of his fiancé's friends, oh, and he's trained to kill with his bare hands."

Brett flashed him a gleefully evil smile.

"Yeah, yeah. You're not telling me anything I haven't already figured out."

Brett shrugged. "Thought I'd give you fair warning." Walking over to a truck parked a few feet from Dev's, Brett reached into the bed and pulled out a lethal-looking ax.

He handed it to Dev and gestured with his chin toward the stand of trees. "Get to it."

Not even aching muscles and blistered palms could keep his mind from wandering back to Willow...and what he planned to do with her once he got her naked again.

WILLOW'S NERVES WERE stretched to the breaking point. She kept waiting for Dev to show up, but so far he hadn't.

She was distracted, and today was not the day for that. There was too much going on. She was behind on the country star's dress—it was supposed to be ready in less than two weeks. The problem with the entire project was that she'd quickly lost interest in it. The entire thing had morphed into a spectacle, the kind of gown that would make her the center of every gossip blog.

And while that should have thrilled her—because her name would be attached to all that free publicity—the dress no longer felt like her own. And she couldn't figure out how to find the spark she'd lost.

Not that it mattered. She had a deadline and a bride who expected a finished product, so she'd make it. Even if it meant pulling several long nights and calling in a few reinforcements. While she tried to do most of the sewing herself, she did have several talented seamstresses who helped when she needed them.

Although today wasn't the day for that, either. The appointment schedule had already been full for the afternoon, but when a bride from Charleston arrived with a last-minute disaster, Willow didn't have the heart to turn her away.

The dress she'd ordered from another shop had arrived in the wrong size and style and no one had noticed until it was too late to fix. The poor girl was in tears explaining to Macey, Willow's business partner, that she needed a brand-new dress in two weeks.

Macey had shown them to a private salon, settled mother and daughter into plush chairs, served them soothing tea and then called in reinforcements. Willow had taken one look at the bride's tear-stained face and wasn't able to say no—even though she probably should have.

The four of them had set out to find a gown that would fulfill the bride's vision for her wedding day while also being immediately available off the rack.

Most of the dresses they carried were samples, designed to be tried on and then ordered in the desired size.

But for the few who were in a hurry to marry, they did keep a small selection of dresses available for immediate purchase.

Unfortunately, the more dresses they tried on the unhappier the bride became. Not that it was easy to tell. She tried so hard to hide her disappointment, but Willow noticed.

And after learning the girl's fiancé was a soldier set to be deployed in a few weeks Willow knew there was nothing left to do. She couldn't send this poor girl down the aisle in a dress she didn't love. Those were memories she'd never be able to get back. Willow would do whatever she had to in order to make this girl's dreams come true.

And her decision was rewarded when the bride flung her arms around Willow's neck and sobbed uncontrollably at her offer to design something for her.

They talked about what she wanted the gown to look like, took measurements and found a ready-made gown that could serve as the base of Willow's design. That would save some time.

When the girl left, she was beaming, and it was her mother's turn to hold back tears as she thanked Willow and Macey profusely for fixing the disaster...and saving her daughter's perfect day. For the first time in several months, Willow's chest swelled with excitement, happiness and pride.

This was why she'd gotten into designing wedding gowns in the first place. To celebrate true love...even if she hadn't been able to find it for herself.

And why did her thoughts immediately conjure up a vision of Dev kneeling before her, looking up through heavy-lidded eyes as his mouth made her quiver?

To hide her flaming cheeks and wayward thoughts, Willow fingered the soft silk of the gown they'd chosen. Without looking up at Macey, she said, "At least she wanted something fairly simple."

"Simple?" Macey's voice squeaked. "An intricate crystal band down the center of her back is simple?"

"Sure, when the rest of the gown is elegant and requires little more than a few strategically placed drapes of material. I can cut out the back of this gown and sew in the embellishment without a problem. I've already got a piece I think will work perfectly. Besides," Willow shot her friend a glance, "I didn't have the heart to tell her no."

"Yeah, neither did I. Why do you think I called you in?"

"We're a pair of softies."

"Of course we are…we sell wedding dresses."

Willow was actually excited about the project. Maybe it was being needed. Or the fact that, even without meeting the groom, she instinctively knew the couple was deeply in love. She'd seen enough brides over the years to spot the fakers.

This girl had been real.

The bell out front rang. Macey left the workroom to help whoever had walked in. Willow stayed in the back, slipping the dress over the naked form standing next to her worktable.

She stepped back and stared at it, distracted by the images flipping through her head as she reached up to a high shelf for a clear plastic box that held strips of hand-beaded lace. It caught on the edge of the shelf and wobbled precariously. Just as it was about to tip and come crashing down on her head, an arm shot past her and plucked it out of the air.

Whipping around, Willow sucked in a breath. Dev stood in the center of her workroom, his wide hands stretched around the container.

He should have been out of place, pure masculinity surrounded by beads and baubles and everything white. Instead, he looked perfect and completely at ease.

The dark suit he was wearing stretched across wide shoulders as he leaned toward her worktable and set the box down.

"You should be more careful."

"What are you doing here?"

Gone was the rough and rugged man she'd seen last night at the diner. The devil from the party was back, slick and sophisticated with a dangerous edge that made her heart beat just a little faster.

Which was the real man?

"I came by to see you. So we could talk."

Adrenaline shot through her blood. She'd vacillated all day. Did she really want to listen to what he had to say, or did she want to send him packing…as she knew she probably should?

Her mouth wouldn't open and tell him to leave. Not this time. Instead, she watched warily as he paced around her domain. This room was her sanctuary, one of the few places where she felt free to explore and create, to be who she really was.

Long fingers trailed across the bolts of fabric that

lined one wall. He picked up a handful of crystals and let them sift through his fingers.

For some reason, watching him made her body tighten and ache.

"You said there were things we needed to talk about."

He jerked his gaze to hers and then away, but his eyes kept track of her as he continued to prowl through her space. He reminded her of a tiger at the zoo, all sinewy muscle and strength contained behind bars that gave people a false sense of security.

"I never touched Rose."

Whatever she'd been expecting, that hadn't been it. "What?"

He finally stopped, squaring his body to face her. The room separated them, but she could feel the slam of his eyes against hers. "I never touched your sister, at least not the way you think I did. We kissed a time or two, long before I met you. I was never interested in her. Hell, she was never interested in me. We were too alike to be attracted to each other."

"Then…what? What are you trying to tell me?"

Dev stalked closer, the heat of his gaze tracking down her body before returning to her eyes. "Rose used me. She told everyone we'd slept together because she knew they would believe it. She wanted out of her marriage, Willow. She was desperately unhappy and too young to see another way to escape the situation she'd landed herself in. Marcus was demanding and domineering."

"What?" she squeaked. What was he talking about? Marcus had loved Rose. Sure, he'd been a little possessive of his young wife, but he'd been right to worry that her wild streak wasn't completely gone.

She would have known if her sister was being abused. Wouldn't she?

"He was stifling her. Telling her where she could go. Who she could see. What she could do. He controlled the money. He controlled everything. She tried to leave him, but he wouldn't let her go. He found her and dragged her home."

"Why didn't she call the police?" Willow's anger fell off into a choked whisper. "Or me?"

"The police couldn't help. He never laid a hand on her, not even when she kicked him out of their bedroom. And what could you have done? You were a seventeen-year-old kid, Willow, with your own worries and life."

"But she's my sister, Dev. I would have helped her however I could."

"Yeah, you would have. Which is probably why she didn't tell you." He reached out and ran his thumb along the ridge of her cheekbone. "I knew she had a plan for getting away, I just didn't realize I featured in it until it was too late. She tried to seduce me. I turned her down flat. By then I'd been knocked silly by you, and there was no way I was going to sleep with your sister."

Willow sucked in a harsh breath. Her gaze darted around his face, searching for some proof that he was telling the truth. She wanted to believe him but wasn't sure that was wise.

Was she blinded by lust and willing to accept anything the slick-tongued man said?

"Why didn't you tell me?"

"I was a little preoccupied with trying to figure

out where the hell I was going to live. My grandfather kicked me out the minute he heard. Even he didn't question whether or not it was true. Why would you?"

"Oh, Dev." The words came out as a moan. Her chest ached.

"Don't you dare."

"What?"

"Feel sorry for me. If I'd done things differently—been less like my dad and more like my grandfather—then maybe…" He shook his head. "But I wasn't. I pulled every stunt I could. I was angry and desperate to prove to everyone I didn't care what they thought of me."

He looked away from her, but not before she caught a glimpse of his pain. The sight of it extinguished any lingering doubts.

He wandered the room, his movements restless.

"Everyone expected the worst from me and it was just easier to give them what they wanted. I was too busy thumbing my nose at the world to think about the long-term consequences of what I was doing."

"You were a kid."

He speared her with the harsh glitter of his gaze. "I was an adult, old enough to know better."

She expected him to close the gap, to finish what he'd started last night now that she knew the truth and the past wasn't a wall standing between them. Instead, he shook his head.

He turned away from her and headed for the door.

"Wait. What are you doing?"

"Leaving."

"Why would you do that?"

He shot her a glance over his shoulder and shifted on his feet. For the first time, Willow realized he was nervous. That shocked her.

"You deserved the truth. It never occurred to me that you thought I'd left you and gone to her. If I'd known…"

His mouth twisted. His eyes filled with concern and…regret. He was worried about her. She had family, although her parents had moved to the Georgia coast several years ago for the sunshine and sand. She had friends—several women she counted as close and knew would be there for her if she ever needed them. But she'd been on her own for a very long time—design school, establishing a business and all the sacrifices that went along with it.

She couldn't remember the last time someone had been concerned about her.

"Don't go," she found herself saying.

Dev's body stilled. The tension that had been tightening his muscles slowly leaked out. The sharp line of his shoulders rounded. With deliberate movements, he turned back to her.

He stood there, his hard, masculine body framed by the utter femininity of her workroom. She couldn't stop herself. Her eyes dropped to the ridge pushing hard against his fly. And she remembered. The feel of him against her, inside her. She wanted more.

Although nothing had changed. Maybe some of their history had been revised, but Dev hadn't changed. Not really. Instinctively, she knew that he was still a loner. Sinful. Dangerous. And he could still hurt her.

But she couldn't let him go. Maybe this was her chance to discover her own sensuality. To let him show her just how desirable she could be. To revel in the buzz of electricity that snapped between them. She'd never felt that with anyone else.

Unlike before, she had no girlish notions about what was happening. This was about right now and nothing more.

She realized she was staring at his straining fly, hunger and heat crashing through her. Her face flushed. Slowly, she raised her eyes to his, licking her lips.

Dev's sharp intake of breath and the pressing weight of his gaze pinned her to the floor. She wasn't sure she could have walked away even if she'd wanted to.

With sinewy grace, he pushed away from the door and stalked closer. He looked down into her upturned face. His eyes were dark and this close she could see the emotions roiling beneath the surface, ones she knew instinctively he wanted to keep in check.

Slowly, he reached for her, running a single finger over the curve of her jaw.

"This is your chance to tell me to get lost. Tonight there are no masks, no past, nothing to hide behind. Just me and you and the craving that's always been there between us."

Two nights ago she'd made a reckless decision and done something foolish, let this man into her bed and her body. She could tell herself that if she'd known who he was, she never would have let him touch her.

But today her body called her ten kinds of liar.

"I'm sorry." The apology slipped out before she even knew she was going to say it.

He didn't pretend ignorance. "You keep saying that, but you've done nothing to apologize for."

"Maybe not, but I feel responsible."

"For something your sister did ten years ago?"

"For believing the worst of you for ten years."

His lips twitched, not with humor but with surprise.

"That apology I'll accept."

The pad of his thumb traveled softly across her skin, gliding over her bottom lip and pulling it open. "But I'd rather have something else from you."

8

ONCE AGAIN DEV was following Willow as she walked into her house. Only tonight there was nothing between them but overwhelming need.

Her hips swayed and she threw him a glance over her shoulder to make sure he was still there. Dev could read the hesitation that still lingered beneath the heat. It bothered him, but he had no idea what to do about it.

The realization that telling her the truth about the past hadn't dislodged whatever concerns she had about this made his stomach tighten. But not enough for him to put a stop to what was going to happen.

He wanted to touch her again…more than he wanted to breathe.

So he'd take what she was willing to give him and worry about the rest later.

He followed her inside. Just like that first night, he didn't bother to look around her place. Who cared how she decorated? He couldn't tear his gaze away from her. How could she not know just how tempting she was?

But she didn't.

And that only made him want her more. Made him want to show her in every possible way just how sexy and beautiful he found her.

Instead of heading straight for the stairs, Willow slipped into the kitchen. Light flooded the room. She stopped in the middle of the space. Dev took advantage, slipping up behind her and wrapping his arms around her waist.

She was tall, but he was taller. Even in the heels that she loved, she fit perfectly tucked into his body. Her head rested against his shoulder, at just the right angle so that he could curve around her and find the fragrant spot where her neck and shoulder met.

The elegant slope of her back pressed to his chest, her rear snuggled around the throbbing erection that was his constant companion when she was near.

God, she felt so good.

Which is probably why he didn't realize that her body was strung tight with tension until his hands slipped over her stomach and up her sides.

She quivered, but not in response to him. The fine tremor coursing beneath her skin wasn't a reaction to his touch...it was something else.

His head—the one residing between his ears instead of beneath his fly—kicked in. "Willow? What's wrong?"

Dev took a step away from her, thinking she must have changed her mind, the hesitation he'd sensed finally coming to the forefront.

But her soft sound of protest and the way she reached behind to grab on to him and keep him close told him that wasn't the case.

Pulling him with her, Willow took several steps toward the sleek table sitting off to the side of her kitchen. The graceful column of her throat bent, dragging his attention down with her.

Dev sucked in a hard breath, finally seeing what she'd already noticed. The glossy surface of a photograph reflecting back at him from the center of her kitchen table. No doubt she'd noticed it immediately because this was her home and she'd recognize the slightest detail out of place.

He'd been too preoccupied with the need to get his hands on her.

Dammit. Anger swelled hard and fast inside him, blocking out everything else.

His hands tightened on her waist and he tried to pull her away. Not that a simple photograph could harm her...but the message sprawled across it in bloodred letters definitely could.

Every muscle in his body tensed for a fight that probably wouldn't come. There was no way to lash out at whoever had threatened Willow.

But the single word—*whore*—wasn't what really bothered him, not that it wasn't bad enough. The real problem was the photograph beneath the writing.

It was from last night. Willow's head was thrown back against the wall in the darkness of the alley. Her eyes were closed and her mouth was open in ecstasy. Several buttons on her shirt hung open, revealing the lacy edge of the bra that matched the panties he still had.

Her skirt was rucked up around her hips, although nothing was visible, at least not to the camera. His head and shoulders were in the way. Even now the memory of her taste burst across his tongue, making his mouth water for her again.

But he pushed the response away.

Someone had watched them.

Not just watched, but taken pictures. And then broken into Willow's home to leave her…what? A threat? An admonition? A warning? Against him.

Grabbing her by the waist, he tried to push her toward the front door. "I'm taking you to my place. I'll come back and deal with this when you're safe."

"No."

She didn't bother with any further argument, simply dug in her heels and dismissed his request out of hand. That wasn't going to work for him.

"Whoever did this could still be in the house, Willow. Please."

Slowly, she turned to face him, putting her back to the sickening message. Instead of the fear that he'd expected to see, her eyes were full of righteous anger and a bone-deep determination.

"I wish they were still here so I could smack the bejesus out of whoever thought this was funny."

Pointing behind her, he said, "That's not a joke."

Whatever it was, a prank wasn't even in the galaxy of possibilities.

Stepping around him, Willow reached for the phone and dialed a number. She said, "Sheriff Grant please. This is Willow Portis and I need to report someone's broken into my home. No, nothing's been taken. At least not that I've noticed yet." She listened for several seconds before nodding her head in a short, quick motion. "Thanks. I'll be waiting."

"No, you won't. Call back and tell Grant to meet us at my house."

Her soft, lush lips pulled into a tight frown. She glared at him. "I'm not going anywhere, Dev. The sheriff's going to want to take a look around. If you want to leave, feel free."

No way in hell. "I'll wait for him, then. I want you out of here. Someone broke into your house and left you a threat."

It was her turn to point. "That's hardly a threat."

Dev's eyebrows slammed down over his eyes. Frustration and fear churned into a poisonous mix in the pit of his stomach. His hands clenched into useless fists at his sides. Why was she being so damn stubborn?

"It sure as hell isn't an invitation to a tea party."

A sound wheezed out of her throat, a combination of anxiety and laughter. Her shoulders finally slumped, losing that ramrod stiffness. It had been just as much of a disguise as the mask she'd worn a couple of days ago, a comfortable facade hiding the worry she was feeling.

Dev wanted to wrap his arms around her and hold her tight, but he wasn't sure she'd appreciate the gesture so he held back.

"No, I don't suppose it is," she said. "I never liked tea much, anyway. More of a coffee girl."

He wanted to argue further, but the sound of a siren in the distance made the point moot. Damn, Grant was fast.

Turning on her heel, Willow headed to the front door to wait for him. The police cruiser sped down the street, painting the neighborhood with revolving red and blue. The effect was as sure as a stone being dropped into water. The ripple of doors opening down the street in the wake of the car as it shot past was inevitable.

Willow groaned and slumped against the frame of her open front door. "Great, something else for everyone to gossip about. Why did he have to use the siren? I'm fine."

There was no love lost between Dev and Sheriff Grant. There'd been a time when Grant had ridden his ass, popping up in a constant quest to find something damning—drugs, open alcohol containers, proof that he was no better than his father.

Dev had resented the assumption and the constant scrutiny. At the moment, though, he had to grudgingly admit that the man was good at his job. He appreciated that Grant hadn't wasted any time getting over here. The sooner this was settled the sooner he could get Willow away from danger.

Grant stepped from his vehicle, turning off the siren but leaving the lights whirling. He looked Dev up and down, his mouth pulling into a forbidding frown.

"Warwick." How could one word be infused with so much animosity?

But Dev refused to rise to the bait. He was no longer a rebellious twenty-year-old, bent on breaking every rule. And he needed Grant to do his job right now more than he needed an argument.

"Sheriff." Dev held out his hand. "I appreciate you getting here so quickly. I tried to convince Willow to leave, but she wouldn't. I don't think anyone's still in the house, but we didn't really check."

Something flashed behind the other man's eyes, but Dev couldn't quite figure out what it was before it disappeared again. Nodding his head in understanding, Grant asked them to wait outside while he looked around the house. Dev was all too happy to oblige, although it did irritate him that Willow didn't bother to argue with the sheriff when she'd been quick to tell him no when he was the one trying to protect her.

Drawn by the spectacle, neighbors flooded into Willow's front yard.

"Willow, are you all right?"

"What happened?"

Dev took a step away from the knot of people forming around her. Most of them ignored him, although several shot him calculating glances, no doubt trying to figure out just what he'd been doing at Willow's house.

She smiled, the twist of her lips a little brittle and tired as she assured everyone that she was okay. She'd only mentioned the photograph to Grant. To everyone else she just said her place had been broken in to.

The response from her neighbors was a mixed bag—horror, indignation and a little apprehension. It was inevitable that they'd go home and check the locks on their own doors twice tonight, wondering if there was a serial burglar and their house would be next.

Dev didn't think so. The message on that picture had been for Willow. This was personal.

But he had no idea why. And that's probably what bothered him the most. Who would want to hurt Willow? She was the sweetest woman he'd ever met. Everyone in town had to know that she'd do anything for anybody. Hell, he'd already received several warnings against hurting her, some from people he didn't even know.

Dev watched as she dealt with everyone, calming fears and reassuring the cluster of people even though she'd been the one to have her sense of security violated.

"It seems like everyone in the neighborhood is here." A soft voice sounded at his elbow. Dev's body jerked. He hadn't realized anyone was paying any attention to him.

Glancing down, he was surprised to find Erica Condon next to him. Her posture mirrored his, her focus on the knot of people around Willow just as his had been.

"It does. Do you live close by?"

Nodding, she gestured across the street and a couple houses down. "That's my parents' house, although it's mine now. They both died a few years ago."

"I'm sorry."

"Don't be. I'm not." Dev frowned. What was that supposed to mean? But, before he could ask, she changed topics as if she'd been talking about nothing more important than the weather. "What happened?"

"Someone broke into Willow's house."

"That's unusual. We don't have a lot of crime in Sweetheart, and this is a good area."

"No place is perfectly safe."

"True, but summer's usually when we have the most trouble, when the rental cottages out by the lake are full of outsiders."

Dev shrugged. That might be true, but he probably knew better than most just how much trouble an insider could cause in Sweetheart if he really wanted to. But either way, that wasn't the point. Not that he intended to tell Erica.

She was nothing more than a nosy neighbor.

Grant's silhouette filled Willow's front door. Despite being in his early forties, the man was still formidable. Dev supposed that was a good trait to have in a sheriff.

Taking the cue, the knot of people who'd formed began to drift away, leaving Willow so that she and Grant could talk.

Without a word, he fell into step behind her as she crossed the lawn and walked up the four steps to her porch.

Grant didn't pull any punches. "Don't think anything's missing, but I'd like you to take a look anyway, just to be sure. The picture's obviously a message, although you might have a better idea what it means."

Willow shook her head. "I have no idea. But…" She glanced at Dev out of the corner of her eye. "You should probably know it was taken last night in the alley close to the diner."

Grant's mouth thinned, but he nodded. Cool gray eyes swung to Dev. "I suppose you're the guy?"

He didn't bother to explain. Stepping behind Willow, he wrapped an arm around her waist and laid his hand possessively across her hip, pulling her back against his body. She stiffened, but didn't try to break free.

"Yes."

"I won't give y'all a lecture about public indecency."

"I appreciate that."

"But y'all should be more careful next time." Returning his focus to Willow he continued, "I'll file a report, but there's really not much I can do. I'll take the picture and dust it for prints, although it'll be a while before we get anything back…assuming I can find some."

"Thank you," Dev said, holding his hand out to the

other man. "Willow will be at my place if you find anything."

"No, I won't."

Both of them turned to stare at her. She crossed her arms over her chest. Dev didn't think she had any idea that the posture pushed the swell of her breasts high against the cut of her shirt.

All the desire he'd suppressed came rushing back with a hard ache that nearly had him gasping. But the challenging glitter in her eyes told him she wasn't interested…at least, not at this precise moment.

She was braced for an argument, and he had no problems giving it to her. At least it was an outlet for the passion thumping just beneath his skin.

"Yes, you will. It isn't safe for you to stay here, Willow."

"I will not be run out of my home, Dev. While I'll admit I'm a little unsettled that someone got in here, if they'd wanted to hurt me they could have just waited and attacked when I came home."

"Maybe they were planning to, until I showed up."

"We would have heard them leaving, Dev. No one was here. But it's possible someone is watching, and I refuse to slink away with my tail tucked between my legs. I won't give them the satisfaction."

Dev's eyes narrowed, evaluating her and trying to determine just where the chinks in her armor were so he could exploit them. Over his years of negotiating with potential clients, he'd gotten very good at discovering which buttons to push to get the results he wanted—it was one reason his business had become so successful.

But before he could act on what he saw, Willow said, "Don't even think about it."

"About what?"

"Trying to convince, argue or cajole your way into getting what you want. I'm not leaving, Dev, and there's nothing you can say to change my mind." She swung her gaze to Grant who'd stood by silently and watched the entire exchange. "Or you. I know how to call if I need help."

Obviously realizing that whatever he said would be a waste of breath, Grant nodded. "Don't be stupid. Anything feels out of place or off, you call me. Don't worry about interrupting or bothering me. This is my job, Willow, and I'd rather rush over and investigate every strange bump than get a call that something terrible has happened."

He pulled out a card, wrote a number on the back and handed it to her. "My cell number. Use it."

Willow stared down at the tiny square of white for a moment before taking it. "Fair enough."

She started to turn to walk the sheriff out, but Grant stalled her. "Warwick, why don't you come out to the cruiser with me. There are a couple things I'd like to talk to you about."

Willow's eyebrows slammed down. "Don't you look at me that way," Grant countered before she could protest. "You said your piece and we're both going to let you make your own decisions, but that means you don't get to argue about this."

Her shoulders rose and fell on a heavy breath. "Fine," she ground out between clenched teeth, but turned away instead of saying more.

Grant gestured Dev forward, following him back out to the driveway. Dev paused beside the car. Grant reached inside and the whirling colors stopped, plunging them both into a sharp darkness. It had gotten late while they'd dealt with all the crap and it took a few moments for his eyes to adjust to the loss of light.

But when he did, he could see the other man staring grimly at him.

"You staying tonight?"

"Of course," he answered. Even if she made him sleep on the sofa there was no way Dev was leaving her alone.

Grant just nodded.

"You hurt her and you'll have me to answer to. And we both know how much of a pain in the ass I can be when I want to. I can make every moment of your time here in Sweetheart miserable."

"What is with everyone? I have no intention of hurting her."

"Why would anyone suspect you didn't? Ten years ago you ruined her sister's marriage and fled town instead of sticking by Rose's side to help her deal with the mess you made."

Dev's jaw tightened. A few weeks ago he would have said he no longer cared what anyone in Sweetheart thought about him—or what had happened. Apparently he'd been wrong.

It bugged the shit out of him, but he was under no illusions that anyone would be interested in the truth now. They hadn't been back then, and nothing had changed. Everyone expected the worst and saw what they wanted.

"Rose made that mess all on her own. And there was

no way I could stick around even if there'd been a reason to. My grandfather kicked me out and told me he never wanted to see my face again. So I left."

Grant's hands clenched tight on the top of the open car door standing between them. His knuckles went white with tension.

"Don't ruin Willow the way you did Rose."

"I have no intention of ruining anyone." Dev wanted to choke back a reassurance—this man didn't deserve it—but it escaped anyway. "Willow's special. Always has been. I'm not stupid. Or blind."

Grant's hold eased, the blood rushing back into his abused fingers. The man studied him with the sharp eyes of someone who'd seen a lot and had developed the ability to separate fact from fiction.

Dev stood, accepting the scrutiny. Even as it bothered him, he realized Grant was only trying to protect Willow.

Finally, Grant nodded and folded down into the driver's seat. Reaching for the door, he said, "I'll give you a call if we find anything." Dev supposed that was the closest he was going to get to acceptance.

He'd lived in the South, around possessive, protective men, long enough. He could read between the lines. Should Forensics find anything, Grant wouldn't be calling Willow…he'd be calling Dev.

He just hoped Willow never found out.

9

WILLOW MOVED THROUGH the kitchen, trying not to let her attention stray to the table where the photograph had been waiting. She wasn't going to let anyone chase her from her own home.

It was late. She was hungry. And no doubt Dev would be, as well. Feeding him was the least she could do considering he'd stuck with her through everything.

The night had definitely not gone the way either of them had hoped.

She sighed, trying to push her own disappointment away, and stirred the strips of chicken, bell pepper and onions she'd thrown into a pan. Tortilla shells were already heating in the microwave, and bowls of lettuce, tomatoes and cheese waited on the island countertop behind her.

She didn't even hear him approach. Her first warning that Dev had come back inside was his hands wrapping around her waist from behind and pulling her against his body.

Knee-jerk reaction had her stiffening, but even before her mind could register who was holding her, her body was relaxing with recognition. Apparently it didn't mind that she was miffed at him for ganging up on her with Sheriff Grant.

Stupid hormones.

"Sit," she ordered, trying to muster up a glare for his benefit. The knowing smirk that teased his lips said she hadn't quite pulled it off.

Although he did step back and pull out one of the chairs around her dark wooden table.

"I'm not much of a cook," she said in a tone that rang with apology.

"If you say 'I'm sorry' I'm going to leave," he warned. "I don't care if you can cook. I didn't ask you to feed me."

"I know, but I needed something to do."

Silence settled over them, heavy with unspoken words. She didn't want to talk about the photograph, and he was obviously aware of her reluctance. She turned away, reaching into the cupboard to pull down two plates. His wooden chair creaked. An unexpected crackle of awareness shot across her skin. Devlin Warwick was sitting at her kitchen table. Three days ago that had been so far out of the realm of possibility as to have been laughable. Now her body buzzed with the low hum of constant awareness and need.

"I would have taken you somewhere for dinner. Gotten you out of here, at least for a little while."

"I didn't want to go anywhere."

"Because you don't want to be seen with me." His voice was low and soft. It was a statement, not a question.

That bothered her.

"Surely you know that's not it," she protested, setting her hips against the hard edge of the stove. From across the room she watched him. The buzz intensified, becoming a sharp ache.

As she watched, Dev morphed. His eyelids dropped down. His eyes glittered at her with promise and heat. Her body responded.

"Stop."

"What?" she asked, her voice gone breathless.

"You keep looking at me like that and it'll be a long time before we eat anything."

Without turning, Willow reached behind her and flipped a switch, turning the burner beneath the pan off.

Dev groaned low in his throat and started to surge up, but a quick shake of her head stilled him.

Willow reached up and found the pins holding her hair in a knot on her head. She slipped each of them free until it all tumbled down around her shoulders.

Dev sprawled back in his chair, spreading his legs wide. The length of his erection strained against the fly of his jeans. She wanted it, and the oblivion only he could give her.

From somewhere deep inside, her inner vixen woke and stretched. What was it about this man that made her feel so desired, that made every look seem erotic? He called to pieces of her soul that even she hadn't known existed…always had.

Slowly, she closed the space between them, reaching up to flick open the buttons on the oversize flannel shirt she'd thrown over skintight leggings.

"Do you have any idea how good you look right now?"

She answered honestly. "No."

"Don't get me wrong, I'm a sucker for those ankle breakers you like to prance around in. And those short little skirts. But that…" His eyes skimmed across her body. "Makes me want to burn everything you own and leave you with nothing to wear but my shirts."

Her sharp intake of breath had the heat in his eyes flaring higher. She should protest, tell him he was an idiot. But she wouldn't. She'd never been one of those women who wanted to be owned and possessed. She was too independent and strong, but with him…the thrill of possibilities shot down her spine.

She wanted to be his, always had. There was a piece of her that was bothered by just how much power this man had over her. How easily he could coax her into breaking her own rules.

The rest of her was too turned on to care.

Obviously, his dangerous edge was rubbing off on her and she wasn't entirely certain that was a good thing.

Dev shifted on the hard chair, drawing her focus back to the weight of his cock pressing against his fly. Her pulse fluttered and her gaze pulled up to tangle with his. What she saw there stole her breath, made her burn and scared the crap out of her.

She'd seen the same narrow-eyed, hungry expression on one of those nature shows, a sleek panther stalking prey. He hadn't moved, and yet she already felt caught. Out of her depth. Severely outclassed and lacking in the skills necessary to escape whatever was coming for her.

But beneath that was a thrill, a burst of endorphins and adrenaline.

Her muscles bunched, and even she wasn't sure if it was to run. But as the possibility occurred to her, she realized it was way too late for caution.

Crossing the space to him, she stepped between his open thighs. His wide hands settled around her waist, holding her still. His head fell back against the curved slats of her kitchen chair. His hooded gaze swept across her, caressing her and sending a flare of heat through her body.

But she wasn't content to just stand there. Not tonight. Pushing against his hold, she climbed right up into his lap, wedged her knees along his hips and sank down onto him.

"We should go upstairs." His fingers tightened around her waist, as if by the sheer force of his will he could hold her a little apart.

Willow shook her head. Hands bracketing his face, she pulled him close. His heat settled deep into her bones, chasing away the chill she hadn't even realized still lurked there. "No. Here. Now. Give me something else to think about whenever I look at this table."

He groaned deep in his throat and closed his eyes for a moment before opening them again and spearing her with those dark blue pools. His mouth was pulled into a grim line, but he nodded, agreeing to give her what she needed even if he wasn't entirely happy about it.

"Thank you," she whispered, closing the gap and sealing her mouth to his. He tasted dark and a little sinful. Which was exactly what she needed right now, something relentless that would suck her down and not let her think.

Willow grasped the hem of her shirt and pulled it up over her head in one quick movement that left her blessedly bare. She hadn't bothered with a bra, and when Dev groaned low in his throat she was glad for the decision.

He filled his hands with her, softly brushing his palms against her aching nipples. But right now she didn't want soft.

Laying her own hands on top of his, she pressed harder. Flexing her hips, she ground her body against the strong ridge of his erection. It wasn't enough, but it was a start.

Dev leaned forward and pulled the heat of her into his mouth. The pebbled edge of his tongue scraped against the distended center of her breast. Willow sighed and arched into him.

Her hair tickled across her back. His hands tangled in the thick mass, angling her back so that he could get a better taste.

Dev ran his lips across her collarbone, taking nipping bites of her as he went. She shuddered.

Her mouth found the skin at the opening of his collar. The taste of him exploded against her mouth, masculine and earthy, sky and sunlight. She needed sunlight right now. Needed him.

Her hands searched between them for his fly. A sound of triumph and appreciation vibrated up from her center when she found exactly what she wanted.

She freed him, reveling in the heavy sound as a groan exploded through his parted lips. Her hips rolled against his, capturing his length between the heat of her hand and the wall of his abs.

He surged against her, silently indulging in the shared sensuality of the caress. Dark eyes glittered at her with promise and the sheen of a fever she understood. He wanted the same thing she did, to have him deep inside her.

Her own muscles clenched hard, wanting. One night with him hadn't been nearly enough. She wasn't sure there was a number that would ever satisfy her, not completely.

Her hand slipped up and down his swollen sex. She could feel the throb, the pulsing urgency echoing deep inside her own body.

"God, I need you. All of you," he ground out.

Wrapping his hands around her waist, Dev lifted her up onto her knees. Her thighs tightened, gripping his body and holding on. The hard press of the chair bit into her kneecaps, but she didn't care. The surface wasn't quite big enough for both of them, but his bracing hold kept her from toppling over.

The change in position dragged her hand away from him. She might have protested, but his mouth found the smooth expanse of her belly and feathered kisses across the surface. Her muscles leaped, contracting at the tickling caress. He leaned forward and nipped at the indent of her belly button, dipping his tongue inside. Burying her fingers deep in the strands of his hair, she held him to her, relishing the way he could make her body respond.

He knew just where to touch. Just want she needed. It was as if he had a direct line straight to her libido. She didn't want to think about the kind of practice that level of mastery required. Or who he'd been practicing on.

Grasping her by the waist again, he set her back on her feet. Her momentary frustration was relieved as she realized just what he was doing. Sure hands slipped the leggings and panties over her hips, thighs and calves. They dropped into a pile at her feet, forgotten as he settled her back against his body.

Her knees wedged on either side of his hips. He didn't waste any time before his fingers dove into the center of her, slipping through the evidence of her desire for him to find the moist heat hidden deep inside.

She groaned. Her hips pitched forward and her head fell back. Dev scrambled to hold her, to keep her from falling. She didn't care. Instead, she leaned against the line of his arm across her back and let herself go off center.

She trusted him to catch her. Even if she didn't fully trust him with everything else.

He worked her, his entire focus completely on her. Her muscles tightened, and when he hit the perfect spot deep inside, her breath hitched.

After several moments of letting him play, she forced herself to pull back to vertical. Her thighs trembled. Her hands gripped the rounded curve of the chair back. She reached for him, wrapping his aching flesh in her tight fist again. But this time it wasn't enough.

Rolling a condom down his thick shaft, she finally let her body sink onto his. Perfectly aligned, she opened herself and took him in, inch by blissful inch. Dev's hands clenched around her hips. She could feel the tension coiling through him as he fought the need to thrust high and deep, to take her in one swift motion that would leave them both intoxicated and delirious.

Part of her wanted him to do it, to take the control away from her and let her just feel. But the rest of her wanted to savor and draw out every moment of the experience.

Her body finally gave, relaxing to take him completely. Her hips bumped his and he settled high and hard inside. Her eyes slipped shut, savoring the sensation of him stretching her, filling her.

She stayed there, poised on the edge of oblivion. Her body trembled. Deep inside, her muscles tightened around him, drawing a gasp.

They were closer even than they'd been the night of the masquerade. There was nothing between them now, nothing to hide behind, and for a moment panic suffused her.

Until his thighs bunched beneath her and he pushed that single centimeter higher and there was nothing but the way he made her feel. Her fingers curved around the nape of his neck, burrowed into the hair there and held on tight.

And then she was moving, the friction of their bodies as deliciously perfect as she remembered. Willow tensed, using her hold on him to lever her body up and then drop back down. Over and over, she let him slip almost to the tip before drawing him back inside her body.

She set the pace, but he joined her, adding the thrust of his hips to bring them even closer together. Pleasure built inside her, a ball of energy ricocheting dangerously and just waiting to explode.

The walls of her sex gripped him, trembling and ready to let go, but not without him.

Willow buried her head against his neck. His mouth found her skin. Teasing teeth scraped against the tendon running up the side of her throat. Ecstasy burst through her, piling on top of the sensation overload.

Up and down, the grinding frenzy of her need increased, tempting her to just let go. Mindless. She was mindless. For once in her life completely uncaring about anything but the way Dev made her feel. Right, wrong, safe, respectable…she no longer cared.

Slipping a single finger between them, Dev found her pulsing knot of nerves and rubbed. Her back bowed, the tight muscles holding him deep rippled and then everything exploded. Pleasure sizzled through her, sharp and freeing. A keening cry ripped from her throat.

Every muscle in her body went liquid. She might have collapsed if his hands hadn't gripped her hips, holding her in place so he could drive deep, taking his own pleasure now that hers was spent.

A groan broke from him, the rattle of it rumbling through her sensitive system. His eyelids fluttered as if he wanted to let them fall, but he didn't. Instead, he stared straight into her.

For a moment the other night she'd wished the masks away so that she could see the delirium and bliss of his release. Tonight she got her wish.

He let her in. Let her see just how completely she unraveled him. He was swamped by sensation, just as thoroughly as she'd been. And there was something unsettling and intimate about that.

Willow's chest expanded and then contracted to tighten into a sharp ache.

She couldn't look away. How could he be the one losing his mind and she be the one on the edge of complete and utter vulnerability?

It was a gift, his openness. And part of her lapped it up, greedily taking everything he was giving her. The rest of her felt as though she was teetering again, on the verge of a very deep chasm. But she couldn't pull back. Couldn't find a way to protect herself. Her defenses had been shattered—torn down by the blow of the break-in and the naked exposure of her release.

So she rode the waves with him, relishing the way he lost himself inside her body, until with a rush of energy he shattered deep inside her. He growled her name, the possessive, delicious sound sending a shiver down her spine.

When his muscles stopped quivering, Willow collapsed onto his chest. Her body slipped across his like summer sunlight, soft and warm. Her mouth found the crook of his neck and her lips latched there, tasting the salt from his skin.

He was still half-hard inside her. Something was beeping.

And she never wanted to move.

Beneath her, Dev stirred. She was completely naked, while the only thing he'd uncovered was his erection. Maybe in a few minutes she'd have enough energy to drag him upstairs and try for round two.

The beep sounded around them again. Dev shifted, canted his hips up so he could reach beneath him and pull out his cell phone.

"Oh, shit," he breathed, horror and guilt flitting across his face before he shut his response down.

After the bare exposure of a few moments ago, the change was as sharp as a fist to the chest.

Wrapping his hands around her hips, he picked her up and put her back on her feet. Cool air brushed across her naked skin and made her shiver.

"I'm sorry, I have to take this." Abruptly he walked away from her, juggling the phone and zipping up his fly.

Willow stood there staring at his retreating back. The soft murmur of his voice might have been soothing…if she hadn't seen the name that popped up on the screen. Who the hell was Natalie? And why was he walking away from her naked body to talk to some other woman?

IT TOOK EVERYTHING inside him to walk away from Willow. Her skin was flushed pink and tempting. Even now he wanted more of her. He wanted to take her upstairs and spend all night exploring her…like he'd done that first night. But this time without any barriers between them.

But he knew his ex-wife well enough to realize that whatever she was calling about couldn't be good.

He skipped past the pleasantries and went straight to the heart, "What's wrong?"

"Nothing, nothing."

"Then why are you calling me, Natalie?" He just wanted to get this over with so he could go back to Willow.

The soft chuckle that slipped down the line made the

muscles along his neck bunch. "Did I interrupt something important?"

"As a matter of fact, you did."

"Who is she?"

"None of your damn business."

"The state of Georgia says otherwise. We're still married so technically you're committing adultery."

His back teeth ground together, but he kept the words he wanted to say from exploding. Another wave of guilt washed across him. He forcibly kept himself from turning to look at Willow. He could hear her, puttering around in the kitchen. Putting her clothes back on. Finishing dinner.

God, he should tell her about the mess he was in. But…it'd only been a few days. They were still dancing around each other. A hard fist tightened inside his chest.

She wasn't entirely sure of him. He'd seen the hesitation play through her eyes when she led him into the house tonight, even after he'd told her the truth about their past.

He didn't want to give her a reason to see the worst in him. He wasn't sure he could take that. Not now. Not after tonight.

Besides, when was the right time to tell the woman you were seeing that you were technically still married? Dev didn't think there really was one.

Especially when in a few weeks the whole damn thing would be a moot point. This marriage was a technicality and nothing more. Rather than give her the opportunity to judge him—and find him wanting like everyone else—he would just fix it.

"I'm not the one living with my fiancé," he grated out.

"Oh, lighten up, Dev. That was always one of your problems. Not everything is a matter of life and death. I was just teasing you. I'd be happy if you could find someone. Surprised, but happy."

"Surprised? What the hell is that supposed to mean?"

"Just that you tend to keep yourself closed off. Always have. That's one of the main reasons we didn't work out."

He was so glad that she'd analyzed their entire relationship and laid all the blame squarely at his feet. Which was bull. He might not have been the best husband—they'd been too young and it wasn't like he'd had a great example to follow. But he hadn't cheated. He'd supported her dreams. Hell, he'd even done the laundry and dishes on occasion.

His teeth ground together. "I appreciate the psychoanalysis, Natalie, but I'm guessing that isn't why you called."

"Nope. Do you have Linda and Ricky's address?"

Dev blinked. "What?"

"Do you have Linda and Ricky's address? Since we have to wait six months for the wedding we've decided to make it bigger. Will is just the sweetest man. I told him I didn't need all the fuss, but he knew I was lying. So I'm expanding the guest list."

"You called me at seven o'clock at night and interrupted…to see if I had an address for your wedding?"

"I didn't know what you were up to, silly."

Dev groaned, screwed his eyes shut and prayed for patience. "That's beside the point."

Her sweet, sunny voice whipped across him. "Well, then what is the point, Dev?"

"You're enjoying this, aren't you?"

The tinkle of her laughter slipped down the line making the tension in his body tighten…and not in a good way. "Little bit."

"No, I do not have their address. You might want to try her cousin Sara."

"I will. Thanks."

"Anytime," Dev growled, absolutely certain he didn't mean it.

Thinking their conversation was done, he started to pull the phone away from his ear, but Natalie's next words stopped him.

"I really do want you to be happy, Dev. You deserve it. I've always worried about you, all alone."

"I'm not alone."

"You are. And I'm not just talking about the fact that you have no family. You don't let people in, Dev. You keep them at arm's length, waiting for them to hurt you. Not everyone will."

This was rich coming from the woman who'd left him. But as much as he wanted to call her on that, somehow he couldn't find the words.

Instead, he said, "Thanks," as a picture of Willow popped into his mind. Not of her naked, although that was a memory he hoped never to lose, but as she'd been in her workroom. Absorbed. Beautiful. Elegant.

God, he was out of his element with her and he had no idea how to find solid ground again. Maybe if he hadn't wanted her for so long he'd have been able to hold back…but there was something about her that stripped away every defense he'd built.

10

It had been a long day. At some point each of her friends had stopped by the boutique to make sure she was okay. Last night there'd been no point in calling to tell them about the break-in. She'd known the whole town would be talking about it by morning, anyway.

And while she appreciated their support and concern, the constant interruptions were wreaking havoc with her productivity.

Willow stared at both of the dress forms in front of her. The dresses couldn't have been more different. Flashy and over-the-top for the country star. Floating, ethereal and understated for the military bride.

There was no question which dress Willow preferred.

Each needed a little more work, but with only a few days to finish them she was finally starting to think she might actually make both deadlines...without the need to forgo sleep for several days.

Panic had stopped being the primary emotion whenever she looked at the dresses, and pride was slowly starting to take over. Even if she personally didn't appreciate the country star's dress, the fact that she'd been able to meet every demand without strangling the woman was enough.

The bell out front sounded. Willow groaned and squeezed her eyes shut for a moment before opening them again with a resigned sigh. Macey had left for an appointment in Charleston several hours ago, which meant she had to handle the boutique. Normally they didn't see a lot of walk-in business in the middle of the week and they'd purposely taken no appointments for the day.

Oh, well. She was at a good stopping point anyway.

Rolling her shoulders and stretching her tight muscles, Willow hollered, "I'll be right out," to the front of the store.

"Don't rush" came back at her in a low, smooth baritone that had need whipping through her.

At some point during his phone conversation last night, Willow had convinced herself she was being an idiot. Who cared that he was talking to another woman? She didn't. Devlin Warwick could talk to whomever he liked.

They weren't exclusive. She didn't have any claim on him. They were just having a good time. Scratching an itch they'd both harbored for years.

She knew what kind of man Dev was and refused to let herself romanticize what was happening between them. He wasn't a permanent fixture in her life. And she was okay with that.

She had to be.

He'd left early in the morning, placing a light kiss on her mouth and telling her that he had to work on the designs for the resort. He hadn't made plans to see her again and she'd had to bite her tongue not to ask him.

Now that he'd shown up, without warning or asking if she was free, she wasn't certain the small thrill racing through her chest was entirely welcome. Oh, she wanted him there, but she shouldn't. Her day shouldn't suddenly get brighter because he'd shown up.

What would happen when he was gone and that never happened again?

Willow walked out of the back to find Dev staring at a display of dresses she'd designed. Her name was scrawled across the wall above them in a scrolling, romantic font. They carried other lines because she wasn't vain enough to think her dresses were perfect for every bride, but hers were the focal point of the entire boutique.

It did something to her to find Dev standing there. Made her nervous, restless and excited. What would he think of her work?

Slowly, he flipped through the silky confections, his head tilted to the side as he studied them. She didn't realize he knew she was there until he said, "These are gorgeous," without even bothering to turn around.

A soft sigh slipped through her lips. "Thank you."

He leaned his back against the column beside him. Considered her the same way he'd studied her designs. Willow shifted on her heels, for some reason feeling unsteady.

"You're very talented."

She scoffed. "I just sew."

"No, you don't."

A pleasant warmth buzzed through her. She tried to cut it off. "What are you doing here?"

"I came to take you to dinner."

Willow raised an eyebrow. "Maybe I have plans already."

"Do you?"

"No, but that's beside the point."

His lips twitched. His gaze swept across her body, taking in the buttoned blouse, knee-length pencil skirt and turquoise-blue heels she'd put on after he left this morning.

There was appreciation in his eyes. A flame kindled deep inside his dark blue gaze making her think she wasn't going to be dressed for very long if he had anything to say about it.

She wanted to walk past him, flip the lock on the door, and find new and inventive ways to use the couches set in front of the three-way mirrors. Which is why she stood still, trying to force down the explosive image and the out-of-control need.

Seriously, she had to get a grip or she was going to completely lose it. And she didn't do that. Ever.

Except around Devlin Warwick.

Dev pushed away from the column, but instead of approaching her and making good on the promise in his eyes, he walked to the opposite side of the boutique.

They carried a line of formal wear for all occasions—bridesmaids, proms, cocktail. Rifling through the racks, he paused and pulled out a seductive red dress. Willow knew everything that hung in the store and recognized it. With a boat neckline and plunging back, from the front it looked elegant and from the back it looked daring.

More daring than anything she normally wore.

"Would you wear this tonight?" he asked.

"I haven't agreed to go anywhere with you. And even if I did…that isn't something I'd choose."

He stalked closer, a frown pulling down the space right between his eyes. "Why not? You'll look gorgeous in it."

"That's beside the point. It's too revealing."

"The dress you wore on Saturday showed more of your body."

"Yes, and look where that got me."

His arm snaked around her waist, dragging her against him. Intensity and power radiated from him so strongly she could almost taste them.

She expected him to push her, but instead he stared at her with those dark midnight eyes and said, "Please."

And for some reason she couldn't say no. Not when every cell in her body felt electrified and alive.

Taking the dress from him, she went to one of the dressing rooms and changed. When she looked at her reflection, she had to admit that he was right. The cut of the dress accentuated her long, slender frame.

She spun, craning her neck to look at the back. She could almost feel the slide of his hand against her skin. It was seriously possible she was going to regret this… but the tingle racing across her skin told her she was also going to enjoy it.

Blowing out a breath, Willow decided it was too late to worry about anything tonight except for the way Dev made her feel.

Coming back out, she tried to clamp down on the thrill at his undeniable reaction. His hungry gaze raced across her body making her a little breathless.

To cover it up, she asked, "Where are we going? I hope you didn't have me dress up for the diner."

"Give me a little credit."

Ushering her out the door, he waited for her to lock up and then drove an hour into Charleston. He pulled to the front of an elegant Italian place she'd always wanted to try. But it was the kind of place you went for special occasions and she'd never had one to share.

Low lighting, secluded tables and dripping candles all set a romantic mood. Part of her wanted to protest that he didn't have to sweep her off her feet. That she didn't want him to.

But she couldn't find the words.

Dev was attentive and funny. They sat across from each other with plates of pasta that almost melted in their mouths and talked—something they hadn't bothered to do up to that point. The buzz of awareness still ran between them, but somehow it had mellowed... wasn't as overwhelming as it had been that first night at the masquerade.

Willow relaxed, enjoying herself, which possibly wasn't a good thing. Dev had taken her out on a date. The kind she hadn't been on in a very long time. And he'd stripped away the facade she'd managed to put back in place just last night.

Without any effort he'd taken this—whatever this was—from just sex and made it something more. He'd made her want these kinds of nights with him, where they talked and shared. Connected on more than just a physical level.

This was so not good.

Willow was quiet as they drove back into Sweetheart. It was late and she rested her head against the seat, staring out the window, letting the scenery lull her as it flashed past.

She'd teased him about his truck that first night, but it was clear that it had plenty of get-up-and-go. It probably could have competed with the Jag he'd said he owned.

Normally she wasn't a speed kind of girl, but with Dev beside her it felt right. Just a little wicked. Until red-and-blue lights flashed in the darkness behind them.

Dev didn't even bother swearing, just eased up on the gas and pulled to the side of the empty road.

Willow leaned forward and watched as Sheriff Grant got out of the cruiser and walked toward them. She groaned and let her head drop back to the seat, twisting so that she could throw a "you've got to be kidding me" glance at Dev.

He simply shrugged, gave her a sheepish grin and rolled down his window to wait.

"What the hell do you think you're doing driving that fast down these roads, Warwick?"

"Don't give me that, Grant. We both know one of the things you love about being sheriff is you get to legally push that car to its limits."

Grant glared through the open window at Dev for several seconds before his body relaxed. "True. What are y'all doing out this late?"

"Went to Charleston for dinner. I'm taking Willow back to my grandparent's place now."

For the most part Willow had only been half-paying attention to the conversation. Dev had broken the law and deserved whatever ticket the sheriff wanted to give him. And since he didn't seem too concerned...

But his last statement had her straightening in her seat.

"What? No, you're not. You're taking me home."

Dev and Grant exchanged a glance, one of those male ones filled with unspoken things that probably would have gotten them both a knee to the groin if they'd said them out loud.

"No, I'm not."

With a nod, the sheriff slipped away from the window. Dev shifted in his seat, turning his entire body to face her. "It isn't safe, Willow. I stopped and picked up a few of your things before coming by the store."

"You did what?" The incredulity nearly choked her. "How did you get inside my house?"

"I used the spare key you left in the hollow rock in your front flower bed. Really, Willow, that thing practically screams 'key inside.'"

She growled deep in her throat. "You went through my things. Packed a bag."

"I've seen you naked, Willow. Repeatedly. It seems rather silly for you to get all indignant that I rifled through your panty drawer."

That hadn't even occurred to her. But now that he'd said it... Her skin flamed with delayed embarrassment.

"While we're on the subject, can I just say that I wholeheartedly approved of your obsession with sexy underwear? Knowing just what you might have on under all those prim and proper clothes you prefer will drive me insane from now on."

Willow sucked a hard breath through her teeth. She didn't want to react, but her body didn't seem to care that he was being a complete Neanderthal. It just wanted him to follow through on the threat and touch her. Now. In his truck. Along the side of the road. Where anyone could drive by and see.

God, what was this man doing to her?

He was making her break every single rule she'd ever given herself. He was calling out the wanton she'd pushed deep down inside and pretended didn't exist.

Glancing behind them out of the corner of her eye, Willow realized that the cruiser was gone. Apparently Sheriff Grant had decided not to bother with a ticket or a warning.

She had two choices. Stand her ground and make him take her home. Or give in to her libido and let him take her to his place and make her feel…anything, everything.

Her libido won.

WILLOW HAD RELUCTANTLY agreed to come back to his grandfather's place. The moment they'd walked through the door he'd distracted them both…and enjoyed every minute of it.

But now that she was sound asleep in his bed, Dev couldn't settle. Without the diversion of the physical awareness snapping between them, he couldn't keep his mind preoccupied. And he was just…worried.

So he'd come downstairs to give his brain something

else to think about, not bothering to turn on the lights. The glowing screen from his laptop was the only illumination in the room.

He'd already done preliminary sketches for the landscape design when he'd submitted his bid package, but of course things changed. Those had been based on the information he'd had on hand and before he'd actually seen the site.

The lake offered some benefits and challenges—easy irrigation for whatever he put in, but the potential for flooding if there was heavy snow up north and lots of run-off. He'd taken several soil samples and was waiting on results from the geological tests required for the kind of massive construction project the resort would be. The test results could change everything, but in the meantime, he was mentally adjusting a few things.

The design program he used was open on his laptop. His feet were kicked up on the scarred coffee table and his entire body had sunk down into the overstuffed warmth of his grandmother's sofa. It hadn't changed since he was five or six. After she was gone, his grandfather had been reluctant to part with it. The thing was ugly and dated, but it was comfortable and Dev couldn't find the will to throw it out, either.

He was busy changing a few of the plant schemes, utilizing more of the natural hardwoods that already surrounded the property, when a soft sound pulled his attention.

Willow stood in the doorway. He had no idea how long she'd been there, but she looked pretty comfortable. Wearing only his shirt.

He was seriously going to have to consider destroying every stitch of clothing she owned.

Her hair was mussed, which never happened. Her skin was flushed from sleep and sex, glowing in the scattered light.

Dev simply stared at her, unable to tear his gaze away. She was beautiful. Of course, she was always beautiful, but this way—rumpled and imperfect—he felt as if he was finally getting a glimpse of *her* instead of the mask she wore for everyone else.

On bare feet, she padded across the room and folded onto the sofa beside him. She leaned close, the sweet and heady scent of her surrounding him.

"What are you working on?"

Reaching around her, Dev attempted to shut the cover on his computer. For some reason he didn't want to show her the work in progress.

He loved his job. It had given him fulfillment when he'd had none. He was good at what he did. It was his place in the world, and for a boy who'd bounced from one bad situation to another without really feeling as if he belonged, that sensation was unexpected and comforting.

He'd never cared what anyone else thought of his career, but Willow's opinion mattered.

The light pressure of her hand stopped him, the lid on his laptop half up and half down.

"Oh, no, you don't. You've invaded my life, toured my workroom like it was a gallery at the Louvre and schemed your way into getting me out of my own house. The least you can do is let me see what you're doing."

They'd bared their bodies and watched each other

as they both lost the world around them to the pleasure they created together. And somehow this moment felt more intimate.

Possibly because it meant more.

This town—and Willow's sister—had taken everything from him once. If he opened up any more would he lose everything again? Rose had just pissed him off and highlighted the damage he'd done to his own life.

Willow had the potential to actually devastate him.

And he'd already been there once before.

With Natalie he thought he'd found someone who understood him. She had come from a rough background, just as he had. They'd both recognized the invisible scars, unable to hide them from each other. That recognition had given them a false sense of kinship, neither of them realizing they were trying to use the other to shore up the damage deep inside until it was too late.

More than anything, Natalie had needed financial stability. And Dev hadn't been able to do that for her. He'd been more concerned with finding happiness, something that centered him and gave him a purpose, than amassing a huge bank account.

There was a part of him that had loved Natalie, even if they'd been absolutely terrible together. He was happy that she'd found someone to give her what she needed.

Why was it harder to let Willow in than it had been to let Natalie go?

Dev's chest tightened. For the briefest moment he thought about telling her to go back to bed. And then she looked at him, her patient, caring eyes punching him straight through the gut.

And his hand reversed directions, opening the screen and revealing the details that he'd been working on.

The fact that she didn't immediately look away to the screen settled some of his tension. Her gaze was steady on his for several moments before she peered at the colorful rendering.

She scooted closer, her legs dropping to the floor as she studied his work. Her quick eyes darted around the screen, taking in the intricacies of his design. She didn't say anything right away, but let it all sink in. Finally, she murmured, "This is fabulous, Dev. I didn't realize you were an artist."

"I'm not. The program does most of the work."

She shook her head at him, raking him with the sharp edge of her gaze. "Not all artists use paper and paint. I should know. You use living things and soil, but the creativity and heart is still clear for anyone who wants to pay attention."

Dev made a sound that could have been agreement or dissent, whichever she was expecting. Inside, his body warmed, not from desire, but from the glow of her praise. She understood. Few people did.

Without warning, her palm landed heavily against his sternum and pushed. Her attention was no longer trained on the glowing screen of his laptop, but squarely on him. The burn was there, deep in her eyes, and his body responded.

This was the bold angel from the first night. The woman who'd thrown him out of her house in a tightly controlled show of anger. She might pretend that she was perfect and compliant, following the rules everyone around her established, but she was strong and fiery beneath the cool exterior.

When she let go, she was a force to be reckoned with. Dev liked that. He respected it, even if on occasion she let herself be swayed by the opinions of others.

"You keep saying this is your grandfather's house, but isn't it yours now? Why haven't you sold it or moved back or changed the furniture?"

It took his brain a few moments to switch gears, especially with the hot weight of her hand pressing against his chest. He wanted to topple her backward, to pull that shirt up so he could run his hands across her soft thighs. Had she bothered putting on the wisp-of-nothing panties she'd been wearing?

Shaking his head, he tried to pull his mind back from the brink. Somewhere, Dev found the right words to answer her question. "The house is mine. I inherited it when he died, although I can't imagine he actually wanted me to have it. I was the only choice."

Willow blinked at him. "Why wouldn't he want you to have it?"

"Well, we didn't exactly part on the best of terms. He was pissed about what I'd done with Rose."

"What he thought you'd done with Rose," she corrected.

He inclined his head in acknowledgment that her words meant more than what was on the surface. Not only did she believe him, she was defending him to someone who was no longer there to care about the truth.

"He didn't believe me any more than the rest of the town."

"But you did tell him the truth."

"I tried."

Slowly, her eyes closed. She kept them that way for a few heartbeats before opening them again. He didn't like what he saw. Pity. Apology.

"Don't you dare. You had nothing to do with it."

"And that makes it better?" Her voice was harsh with the anger she was directing toward herself. Her eyes met his, roiling with a heat that had nothing to do with desire, "Dammit, I want to strangle her for what she did. What she cost you."

Warmth flashed through his chest. He hadn't realized how much it meant to have someone believe him.

To have her support him.

"It's in the past."

"No, it isn't, Dev. I spent ten years thinking the worst of you. The entire town did. Do you know how many people have warned me against you since you came back?"

He made a rude noise in the back of his throat. "I'm guessing pretty much everyone you've talked to."

"This isn't funny."

"I'm not laughing."

"How can you be so flippant about everything? Her selfishness cost you so much. You didn't even return for your grandfather's funeral."

Willow's skin had gone pink and her eyes glittered with fury and exasperation...on his behalf. She was ready to fight for him. Had already been doing it, if he was reading between the lines correctly.

It had been a long time since anyone had thought him worth fighting for.

God, he wanted her. In that moment, the only thing he could think about was getting his hands on her. The soft, welcoming heat of her body surrounding him.

And there was no reason to deny what he wanted.

Flattening his hand over the palm still resting against his chest, he held her to him as he pressed closer.

"You don't have to carry the weight of everyone's expectations and sins on your shoulders, Willow."

"I don't know what you mean."

Of course she didn't. But he could see. How she'd been careful to live her life to atone for the choices Rose had made. And not just what Willow had thought Rose had done with Dev. Rose had always been over the top, pushing boundaries and testing patience. Becoming a Vegas showgirl was just the last event in a long line of outrageous behavior.

Willow had made herself into the paragon of saintly virtue to protect herself and appease everyone else. And she'd done it to make up for her sister's flamboyant excess and disregard for anyone and everything.

When he'd walked into her workroom it had been the first time—aside from when she was mindless with passion—that he'd felt she was really present. That she was wholly relaxed and entirely herself. Not playing the seductive angel or the serious businesswoman. He'd recognized the faraway expression of someone lost in their work…because he wore the same one often enough. She wasn't hiding or pretending. She just…was. And she'd been more beautiful than ever.

But he couldn't explain that to her. He couldn't tell her that he *saw* her, saw beyond the front she put on for everyone else to the pieces she was trying to hide. That admission would reveal too much.

He hadn't wanted the words from her, but she gave them to him anyway.

"I'm sorry."

None of it was her fault and yet the soft, low sound of her voice soothed something deep inside him he wasn't even aware was still injured. He hadn't wanted to acknowledge that it still hurt.

And he couldn't admit that to her, either.

Without thought, he reached up and rubbed the puckered scar on his cheek. Catching himself, he ran his fingers through his hair to cover up the revealing action.

But she saw anyway, her eyes sharpening slightly. The soft pad of her finger skated across his skin, pressing against the scar. She didn't even ask where he'd gotten it. She didn't have to, in order to understand.

Dev closed his eyes for a brief moment, trying to find a calm center in the storm of emotion swirling up inside him. But there wasn't one to find, so he let the storm take over instead.

When he opened his eyes again, Willow was staring at him with the same heat and bone-deep need that was drowning him.

He surged against her, knocking them both back onto the couch. The worn wooden frame groaned at the sudden shift of weight, but he didn't give a damn. The thing could collapse beneath them for all he cared. He probably wouldn't even notice.

Frenzy and heat. Driving need. If he'd stopped to think for a moment, he might have worried that his plucking fingers and demanding mouth could bruise her pale skin. But Willow was right there with him.

The sharp sound of ripping material joined their heavy breathing when she tugged his clothes from his body. Naked skin slipped against naked skin.

"Do you have any idea what you do to me?" he asked, no longer worried about keeping his desperation to himself. Holding himself up on shaking elbows, he stared down into her eyes. "When you're around the only thing I can think about is the way you smell and taste. The heat of your body and how good you feel when I'm deep inside."

Her lips twitched. "That's just good sex."

"No, it isn't. I've wanted women before, Willow. You're different. Always have been. Even when I knew I shouldn't, I couldn't stop from wanting you."

Her arms wrapped around his neck and pulled him down to her waiting mouth.

"Lucky for you, you don't have to."

With a groan, he sank down into her, letting her soft curves take him. It was so easy to lose himself in her.

Until a loud clatter came from the kitchen. Dev vaulted from the sofa, halfway across the room before the sound stopped. Willow squeaked out a muffled yelp of surprise.

It wasn't until later that he'd question the intelligence of bounding into unknown danger completely naked. At the time, all he could think about was protecting Willow.

Instinct kicked in and it was rewarded because when

he reached the doorway to his kitchen it was to find the back door hanging wide-open. And he knew damn well he'd shut and locked it.

11

DEV PULLED DOWN Main looking for a parking spot in front of the hardware store. He'd barely slept, even after Sheriff Grant had left his place. Once again, there wasn't much the man could do, but filing a report at least let Dev feel as though they were doing something.

Grant had tried to reassure him, but it hadn't worked very well. No, whoever was watching Willow hadn't physically harmed them, but that didn't help the tingling tightness at the back of Dev's neck.

He felt helpless, unable to figure out what the hell was going on so he could protect her. And it didn't help that there was no place that truly felt safe, not her house and now not his.

Her studio. At least there she wouldn't be alone and vulnerable. Maybe he'd look at getting a room at the inn until they figured out what was going on.

In the meantime, Brett Newcomb had called early this morning and asked to meet with him at Sonny's Hardware. Dev had tried to put him off, reluctant to leave Willow alone, but she wouldn't hear of it.

The only thing that had finally convinced him to leave was Willow's reassurances that her business partner would be at the boutique with her. He'd checked every room and closet, and double-checked all the locks on the windows and doors of his house before he'd left her standing over his sink putting on her makeup. And he still wasn't entirely happy.

But Willow was stubborn and she'd threatened to go back to her house—alone—tonight if he didn't get his butt to the meeting. So he'd left. What else could he do? Although the tight, uneasy feeling that had taken up residence in his chest wasn't going to go away until he saw her again.

Taking a spot half a block down the street, Dev pocketed his keys and headed to Sonny's.

He didn't understand why Newcomb wanted to meet there, but when the client asked...

"Warwick, glad you could make it."

A hand slapped down on his back and propelled him inside the hardware store.

This was the kind of hometown place that had been in a family for generations. According to the sign, it had been established in 1946.

Rows of shelves towered above his head, touching the twelve-foot ceilings. They were jam-packed with everything a handyman could drool over—power tools, pipe elbows, electrical boxes and an array of nails and screws in every size.

At the front was a long counter, which held an ancient computer and the general detritus of business. But there were also a couple of rickety tables and a sofa that had been old in the '50s, all empty.

Dev figured Brett had called him here so they could talk with the owner about the supplies he'd need when the actual work got under way. Normally, he preferred to order from his own suppliers, but one of the bid requirements had included using local businesses.

Dev had to admit he'd been intrigued by the demand. When most companies were only concerned with the bottom line, the Sweetheart Consortium seemed willing to balance quality and profit with supporting the community.

And it helped that the building was going to be breathtaking. He'd wanted to be a part of it and would have bid on the project even if it hadn't been in Sweetheart.

Dev headed for the counter, but Brett's hand steered him to one of the long aisles instead, pushing him farther into the dusty confines. He tried to ask Brett where they were going, but he just shook his head and gave a conspiratorial smile.

Dev didn't like those kinds of smiles. They usually meant someone knew something he didn't.

The aisle ended and Brett pointed to a door. It was split along the bottom, splinters of wood breaking free and crumbling. The surface was stained with several garish splotches of paint, as if it was used to test for true color. Dev assumed it was a supply closet or storage area.

He was surprised when Brett pulled open the door and a set of stairs materialized. A basement. The staircase was dark, a lightbulb swinging uselessly from the ceiling.

Brett clapped a hand onto his shoulder and directed

him down the stairs in front of him. Unease, an unwelcome echo from last night, tightened the skin at the back of his neck. "Are you taking me down here to drop me into a pit or murder me?" Dev asked, throwing a half joking, half concerned smile over his shoulder.

Brett's lips twitched. And Dev noticed the muffled sound of voices as they got closer to the bottom. They stepped into a dusty room that was just as dark as the staircase. There were boxes stacked everywhere, but through the gloom he could just make out a doorway, a strip of light glowing next to the floor.

This time when Brett tried to steer him, Dev dug in his heels. "What is going on?"

"You'll see," the other man said cryptically.

He'd instantly liked Brett Newcomb when they'd met. Brett was new to the area, so he hadn't been prejudiced by the stories of ten years ago. He was a good businessman, a talented architect and Dev appreciated his ability to cut through bullshit. Even though he'd only known him for a few weeks, he'd already begun to think of the man as a friend.

Now he wasn't entirely certain.

"Trust me," Brett said, nodding toward the door. "You wanna go inside."

Deciding he had nothing to lose—unless Newcomb really was a serial killer—Dev opened the door. And stood dumbfounded on the threshold.

It was the mecca of manhood. There was a long, cherrywood bar along one wall. Several televisions. Deer heads, mounted fish and sports jerseys covered the walls. Trophies—from Little League up to state championships—occupied a huge glass case. And every beat-up recliner or sofa that had been kicked out by a self-righteous wife had come here to die...or be used until it literally fell apart. A cloud of cigar smoke mingled with the scent of grease.

"Holy crap," Dev breathed out. "What is this place?"

"The Eros Lodge. Don't ask about the name, no one's been able to give me a satisfactory answer yet. No women involved and still they went for something froufrou." Brett shrugged and wandered over to the bar where several men sat with huge plates of eggs, pancakes, bacon and sausage in front of them.

"Warwick," someone yelled from across the room. "Glad you could join us. Pull up a chair."

Dev followed the sound over to an older guy lounging in front of one of the humungous TV screens. He gestured to the scarred leather armchair beside him, held together with duct tape.

Shaking his head, Dev wended his way through the space. Had he dropped into Wonderland when he'd walked down those stairs?

Most of the men occupying the cavernous room were older, in their sixties and seventies. But there were a few thirty- and forty-year-olds in suits, eating breakfast and nursing steaming cups of coffee.

He sank down into the chair and groaned at how perfectly the leather reached up and cradled him, wrapping around his body. It might be an eyesore, but the thing was pricelessly perfect.

"I know," the guy who'd called to him said with an understanding smile. "Welcome to the Eros Lodge. I knew your grandfather since we were schoolboys. He loved that chair. Name's Gus."

Dev had a vague recollection of Gus, fuzzy memories from his life here, although he'd been a headstrong teenager and a pissed-off adult so he hadn't really paid attention to who his grandfather's friends were.

"Gus. He talked about you. Nice to meet you."

Gus inclined his head. "You've been sponsored as a legacy. We don't have many rules here, son. The most important one is if you tell any of the women what we have down here, we'll castrate you." Gus laughed loudly, the sound bursting and echoing as others around them joined in.

Dev wasn't entirely certain they were joking.

"You're free to use the premises whenever you like. Marty is the best bartender in town and Nicholas makes the best grits and grills a mean burger. And you can watch the game in peace."

Gus leaned forward, his starkly lined face pushing through the haze that lingered around the place.

"On a personal note, if you hurt Willow Portis you'll have all of us to answer to. She ain't got no family here anymore, but all of us consider her one of ours."

Dev swallowed.

"Grant said you're fighting tooth and nail to keep her safe, though, so we thought you deserved the benefit of the doubt. We've all been headstrong and stupid before. If Willow's forgiven you for what happened, we're willing to let the past go and give you another shot."

The room had gone suddenly silent. He glanced around, realizing everyone was watching him. His mouth went dry. For a moment, he thought about telling this man—a man his grandfather had known and trusted—what had actually happened ten years ago.

But the thought made his stomach tighten. They'd let him in. Accepted him. Even thinking the lies from ten years ago were truth. At least, that's what he thought this whole thing meant.

"The last thing I want to do is hurt her, Gus."

Gus stared hard for several seconds and then finally jerked his head in a single, decisive nod. And just like that, the conversation was over.

Gus stood and walked away. Brett slipped into the chair he'd vacated and began discussing the resort as if there was nothing strange about conducting business in the basement of a hardware store.

And maybe there wasn't. Dev sank down into the discussion, enjoying the intelligence Brett brought to the conversation as they debated the merits of the design changes Dev was suggesting.

Business finished, Dev settled into the welcoming glove of the recliner and said, "I never knew this place was here."

Brett shrugged. "I didn't find out until I'd been in town for several months and proposed to the mayor's daughter in front of the entire town. They're pretty particular about letting people in. They like to protect what they've got going."

Dev's gaze traveled slowly around the space, still unsure exactly what to make of it.

"Have to admit, I was a little pissed when they asked me to get you down here. Until they told me your grandfather was a member." Brett frowned, his cool eyes appraising. "You didn't tell me you grew up in Sweetheart."

Dev's hands tightened around the coffee cup cradled

in his fist. "I don't remember that being a requirement of the bid."

"True, but you might have mentioned it when we first met."

"Why? No one in Sweetheart particularly likes me."

"I'd have to say you're wrong on that. Trust me, I know what this town is capable of doing to someone they don't like. When I first arrived they hated me."

"When I left they thought I was evil incarnate."

Brett took a long drink and studied Dev over the rim of the cup. Lowering it back to the table, he finally said, "Apparently they've changed their minds."

Dev opened his mouth, the familiar protest on his lips, but it never materialized. He'd come to Sweetheart thinking he was here to show the town that they'd been wrong about him and he didn't give a damn what they thought anymore.

But the flood of warmth that suffused him the moment he realized just what this place meant proved him a liar. And maybe there was a part of him that wanted this not to matter.

But it did.

With one simple gesture they'd made him feel welcome…and pulled him right back in. He just hoped he didn't get the welcome mat ripped out from under his feet again.

Dev's cell phone buzzed against his hip, startling him away from the foreboding thoughts. Looking at the screen, he was about to let it go to voice mail when he realized it was Willow's store.

He couldn't stop the twin bursts of bliss and disquiet that jolted through him.

"Hey, beautiful," he answered. "Everything okay?"

"No, it isn't."

Dev jackknifed straight in his chair the moment he realized the voice on the other end of the phone wasn't Willow.

"Who is this? What's wrong?"

"Macey, Willow's business partner. She's fine, but you need to get over here. Now."

WILLOW STARED AT the mess, dumbfounded and...lost. Tiny iridescent beads in every shape and size were scattered across the floor. Bits of lace in varying shades of beige and white fluttered every time someone walked past. They reminded her of the feathers from her wings, floating softly through the air.

There was nothing angelic about what had happened in her workroom.

Someone had torn it to shreds.

If it was just chaos, Willow could have handled that. Putting bolts of material back on the rack on the wall, re-sorting all of her crystals and sequins.

But whoever had done this had gone beyond making a mess. They'd ripped both of the dresses she'd been working on into nothing more than rags.

Both brides were expecting a finished product in little more than a week.

Hot tears prickled behind her eyes. Willow tipped her head back and stared at the bright lights, letting them burn away her weakness. She had too much to do to lose it now.

Macey had been fabulous, offering to contact both brides to let them know what was going on. Willow had told her to promise them she'd find a way to fix this. Possibly by getting hopped up on energy drinks and spending the next seven days without sleep. But they didn't need to know that.

Both brides needed the reassurance that everything would be okay. This wouldn't ruin their perfect days. Willow wouldn't let it. Not even the demanding country star deserved that.

But there wasn't much she could do until Sheriff Grant and his team finished processing her workroom. Given the damage to her business and property, and the previous incidents, there was more he could do this time.

Even though she knew Grant and his team didn't need her help, she couldn't make herself leave, so she'd lodged herself into the corner of the room and was watching.

Hope rushed in, followed by Lexi, Tatum and Jenna. Without a word, her friends circled around her, dragging her into their tight, supportive embrace.

"Are you okay?" Lexi asked.

Ever practical, Hope said, "Of course she's not okay, but she will be."

Tatum held her at arm's length. "You're tougher than you look and we're all here to help any way we can. Just tell us what you need. I'm not great with a needle and thread, but I'll do my best."

Willow's smile was weak and watery, but she gave it to her friends anyway. Looking at the circle of faces that surrounded her, Macey included, she felt the tension inside her chest ease just a little.

These women were her rock. She'd always known

she could count on them for anything, but their unwavering support meant more to her than she'd ever realized.

"I appreciate the offer, but I've seen your sewing skills. They suck. I might let you keep the supply of coffee going, though."

"Done," Tatum said, pulling her back into a tight hug before letting her go again.

A clatter at the door startled them all. Everyone turned to watch as Dev shot into the room. His anxious eyes darted around, taking in the mess and the people before zeroing straight in on her.

Stalking into the chaos, he wrapped her in the comforting heat and support of his arms. Her name whispered against her temple, the single word splintering the fragile hold she had on her own emotions.

She looked up into his dark blue eyes. They were filled with regret, sympathy, sorrow and a bone-deep fury that might have made her shudder with dread if it had been pointed at her.

He dipped his head down, pressed his mouth to her forehead and mumbled, "It'll be okay," against her skin.

The dam that had been holding everything back burst and she completely lost it. He swept her up into his arms and she let him. He carried her somewhere quiet. The world tilted. Lowering them both to the floor, Dev settled her heavily against him.

Burying her head in his shoulder, Willow let it all go. She sobbed against him. Her fists wrapped in his shirt, balling it and pulling him closer. The steady pressure of his hand brushed up and down her back in a soothing rhythm.

He didn't tell her to stop. He didn't try to comfort her. He just sheltered her with his body and held her tight, letting the emotion pour out of her however it needed to.

Willow had no idea how long they stayed there locked together like that, but when the tears were spent and she could finally breathe without a painful hitch, she looked up to find them at the far end of the hallway outside her workroom.

"Oh, God," she groaned, pressing her face back into Dev's shoulder to hide the rush of embarrassment that touched her skin. "I just made a complete fool of myself."

"Cut yourself some slack. You've been through a lot today." Dev's voice rumbled at her, the vibrations slipping from his chest into her own.

An ache that had nothing to do with what she'd lost began to thump in the center of her chest. It wasn't desire—or wasn't *just* desire, since that was always there between them—it was more.

She liked him. She wanted him. She cared about him.

And that was the stupidest thing she'd ever done. But what could she do? If there were a woman alive who could resist Devlin Warwick, Willow would like to meet her. He was sexy and charming with a dangerous edge. Tempting. Kind. A little lost and wounded.

And he'd known exactly what she needed and given it to her.

"Grant said they've got what they need. Hopefully this time whoever's doing this slipped up and left a fingerprint or something."

"I know I locked my workroom before I left last night. I'm anal about security."

"Well, apparently locks aren't enough to stop this person. They've broken into your house, my house and your workroom. Until this is resolved, promise me you won't go anywhere alone."

While part of her wanted to protest on principle, Willow wasn't stupid. The incidents were escalating and this last one had been more than personal. It had been vindictive and destructive.

"I promise."

"Your friends are cleaning up your workroom, although I have no doubt I'm only going to be able to keep you out of there for a few more minutes. Let them help you."

She nodded.

"Let me help you."

A weak smile played across her lips. "Do you have a hidden talent I'm unaware of? Can you sew?"

"Unless you're going for Gothic, with spots of blood, you should keep me far away from needles."

A shudder of revulsion shook her. "God, no blood." Somehow, despite everything, he'd found a way to make her smile. And that was probably more important than anything.

She'd purged the emotions that had been building inside her. The heavy weight crushing her chest was suddenly lifted. And despite everything, she felt hopeful.

"Well, one good thing might come from all of this."

"Oh, yeah, what's that?"

"Now I get to give the country princess the design I wanted all along. For a woman constantly in the spotlight, she has no clue what looks good on her body type."

"That's my girl," Dev said.

Willow looked up into his face. Snuggling in his lap, with approval and pride shining down at her from his dark eyes, she felt warmed through.

And suddenly the moment of happiness she'd found dimmed.

She was in so much trouble. And the danger had nothing to do with whoever was stalking her or the potential damage to her reputation as a designer.

She was falling for Dev all over again. And just as before, she was going to get her heart broken. Only this time she wouldn't have anyone to blame but herself.

12

TONIGHT EVERYTHING FELT different. He felt different. Today had been a game changer. Getting that phone call from Macey, walking into Willow's workroom to find her standing there in the middle of all that destruction…

Never in his life had he been violent. His father, when he'd been around, hadn't had a problem beating the shit out of him for no reason. Dev had been more a lover than a fighter, using his face and charm instead of his fists to get what he wanted.

But in that moment he could have joyfully hurt whoever had left that hunted, injured expression on Willow's face.

Maybe no one else had noticed the cracks that were showing through her facade, the cracks she was trying desperately to shore up, but he had. The moment he'd walked into the room he'd recognized just how close she was to losing it. And he'd wanted nothing more than to give her a safe place to land.

Not just then, but forever. He'd fought the need to whisk her away to someplace safe, mostly because he knew she wouldn't appreciate the gesture. So he'd settled for the silent hallway, as far away as he figured she'd let him get while her design studio was in a shambles.

They'd taken the rest of the day to put everything to rights. He hadn't spent much time with her friends up to that point, but he liked them. Even if they had given him several hard looks and individually found a moment to warn him against hurting her.

What was it with the citizens of Sweetheart? Willow had more people watching over her virtue than the average nun.

But even though it was slightly annoying, knowing she had so many people who cared for her also made him happy.

It had taken some fast talking from him and her friends to convince her there was no reason to start redesigning the dresses tonight. She needed a little rest before she dove into a marathon design session.

So he'd brought her home. To the only one he'd ever really known.

He pulled into the driveway, and for the first time in a long while, instead of seeing the place as a burden he remembered the moment he'd driven up when his grandfather took him in. He'd visited before, but that time he was there to stay and everyone knew it.

Relief had flooded him, but experience and wariness had kept him from showing it. His grandfather hadn't said anything, just reached across the bench seat of his pickup to place a heavy hand on Dev's shoulder. He'd squeezed. It was the silent comfort and reassurance his grandfather had instinctively known that young Dev had needed.

Part of him wished his grandfather was still here so he could find that reassurance again. He had no idea what he was doing—in Sweetheart and with Willow. He'd come here for a little benign revenge and instead he'd fallen for a brilliant, cool, poised and passionate woman who had the potential to turn his life upside down. Again.

He'd promised himself he'd never be that vulnerable again. But he couldn't seem to turn away from her. When she'd looked at him today, those light blue eyes still shiny with tears, as if he was the only person holding her life together...

It had been a very long time since anyone had looked at him that way—as though he was worth something. Like he mattered.

Taking Willow's hand, Dev squeezed it and then jumped out. Striding around the side of the truck, he helped her from the cab.

Her body collided with his, slithering down as her feet found the ground. He reacted, every cell going on full alert.

Dev wanted her. To touch and taste. To fill her up and assure them both that she was safe. But now wasn't the time for that. She'd been through enough today and needed peace.

Unfortunately, he knew the one place that would normally have provided that—her studio—wasn't going to work. At least, not for a little while. So he did the next best thing.

Tugging on her hand, he led her around to the gate

in the side of the fence and pushed it open. The hinges squeaked and the wood creaked. Her small gasp of surprise as she walked into the garden was enough of a reaction to make his chest swell just a little with pride.

"Dev, this is gorgeous. I had no idea it was back here. Did you do this?"

He'd hired a landscape company to keep everything in order, but somehow it hadn't been the same. The bushes were trimmed, the mulch in the proper places. The few late-blooming flowers had been fragrant.

But the moment he'd walked out here that first night it had felt impersonal. Everything was right, but it wasn't his grandmother's garden. So he'd spent his downtime back here trying to capture the elusive element that had been missing.

Willow walked farther into the garden. Slowly, she turned to take it all in. The soft tinkle of the pond in the far corner. The stone bench. The rosebushes climbing up a trellis.

Finally, she turned to him, a beautiful smile on her face. And he realized exactly what had been missing... her. Heart and soul.

She was surrounded by color and the new flowers he'd planted. Autumn crocus, calla lilies, some asters. Most of the flowers wouldn't last much longer, but while he was here, he'd needed to see them. To see the place as it had once been.

If he was honest with himself, by restoring the garden of his memories he'd been saying goodbye. When the Sweetheart Consortium job was finished there'd be no reason to hang on to the house anymore. No reason to stay.

A sharp pain lanced through his temple and he closed his eyes, willing it away.

"I thought you might like to sit out here for a little while. Just breathe."

Willow, polished, contained and utterly sophisticated stood in the center of his domain. She should have looked out of place. But she didn't. She was perfect. Just like the milky-white tubes of the calla lilies off to her left, she held heat and color deep in the center of her soul, only sharing the secret with a very lucky few.

She cocked her head to the side and considered him for several moments. Flicking her feet, she let her designer heels fall haphazardly to the ground. She didn't even watch where they landed, just flexed her toes, letting them crush down into the dirt.

The look of utter bliss on her face was erotic as hell. She stood in the middle of his sanctuary, his fallen angel, perfect, hugely tempting and slightly disheveled.

Crooking her finger at him, she lured him forward. "Show me."

He took several steps toward her. How could he not?

"What?" What did she want to see? How she could drive him to his knees with nothing more than a glimpse of the passion in her eyes? How much he wanted her?

"Whatever you want. I want to watch you work. Show me what you do."

That was not what he expected. "You're going to get dirty."

"If you haven't figured out that doesn't bother me then there's no hope for you."

"Just making sure."

Gesturing her over to a corner of the garden he'd

cleared for some new flowers, he showed her how to prep the soil, pop the small root ball from the waiting pot and transfer the plant to its new home. She dug right in, quickly picking up the mindless rhythm.

They worked side by side for a while. He enjoyed watching her muscles relax and the tension she'd been carrying like a constant companion ease. The silence that stretched between them took the edge off the ever-present need. Dev was surprised to realize that sitting there with her in the quiet twilight was effortless. While he'd meant to give her a space full of much-needed peace, he'd also managed to give it to himself.

Or maybe she'd done that.

Dropping back onto his heels, Dev watched Willow. At least he'd convinced her to go inside and change out of her dress and into something more appropriate. Her long, slender fingers were dusted with dirt. Clumps of it clung to her jeans-clad thighs. The muscles in her arms and back bunched and strained. Her teeth ground together as she fought a particularly stubborn weed that didn't want to let go of its hold.

It finally popped out. The sudden loss of resistance sent her toppling over onto her rear. Not even the surprise of that could diminish the light of triumph in her eyes. She'd won.

Dev couldn't help but laugh at the vision she made, sprawled on her butt in the grass.

Until a mangled clump of dirt smacked him right in the chest.

"You think that's funny?"

"Absolutely not," he said, trying to bite the inside of his cheek and get control of his reaction.

The effort was wasted, though, since he had no intention of letting her projectile go unchallenged.

Stalking toward her, he scooped up a handful of loose potting soil he'd mounded beside the flower bed. Willow wasn't stupid. She knew what was coming and wasn't willing to sit still and take it. She scrambled to her feet, poised to dart away.

But he was faster.

Snatching her around the waist, Dev pulled her close. His mouth nuzzled the spot just behind her ear. Her body responded immediately, relaxing against him.

And then he struck, tugging at the neck of her shirt so he could let the moist dirt trickle down her back. She gasped and squirmed, but he held her tight.

She was driving him crazy. What had started as retaliation quickly backfired on him. The moment he'd touched her he was a goner and the more she rubbed in all the right places...

Wrapping his hand around her jaw, Dev pulled her mouth to his. The moment his lips found hers she stopped struggling to get away from him and started trying to get closer. Her response was immediate and made something primitive swell deep inside him.

His arm wrapped around her waist, pulling her back snug against his chest. He cradled her neck, holding her so he could take the kiss deeper. She sighed and melted into him.

He half expected her to protest when he moved to pull her shirt off over her head, but she didn't. The fences were high and no one would see them here in the privacy of his backyard. But that wouldn't prevent the neighbors from hearing, if they were outside.

She didn't stop him. Instead, she helped him, pulling frantically at the confines of her bra and tossing it away. She barely gave him time to appreciate the tantalizing effect of the see-through mesh and lace before it was gone.

"Have I told you how much I love your underwear?"

Her mouth curved. He felt more than saw her smile. "Not enough to leave it in one piece."

His hands found warm, willing flesh. One hand splayed across the tight expanse of her tummy, pressing her against the bulge straining his fly. The other found the tight buds of her nipples. They thrust against his palm when he dragged his hand over her. Her back arched, seeking more even as her taut derriere ground against him, making him breathless with wanting her.

Suddenly, he needed to see her, all of her, here, where he found his own sense of peace and comfort. He wanted to drag rose petals across her body so that she could feel how soft they were and he could smell and taste them on her skin.

Darkness was falling. Gloomy shadows twisted around them. The only sound was their mingled gasps as they drove each other insane with need.

When Willow pulled away from him, Dev expected her to grab his hand and lead him inside to the first flat surface. Instead, she walked several paces farther into the dusk. Keeping her eyes firmly locked with his, she reached for the fly of her jeans and tugged.

The gentle rasp of metal teeth letting go sounded as loud as a sonic boom in his ears. When she rolled her hips, dropping the denim to the ground he understood just what kind of appeal Eve must have had in the Garden of Eden. Willow was surrounded by the lush green and deep brown, making her skin glow in the pale light.

Slowly, she reached for her hair, letting it tumble down to her shoulders. It brushed against the peaks of her breasts, making his mouth water for the taste of her again.

In one quick burst of motion he was in front of her, his hands filled with as much as he could take. He hadn't even formed the thought to move before they were twined together again.

Her hands tugged at his clothes, pulling his shirt from his shoulders and dropping his jeans to the ground. Somehow they found their way down to the soft layer of grass at their feet.

The scent of jasmine mixed with something wholly Willow. Somewhere in the frenzy, Dev found that elusive moment of tranquility. He brushed the hair back from her face and stared deep into her bright eyes. She didn't say anything. She didn't have to, he could see her clearly, maybe more clearly than anyone else ever had.

She was a mix of so many things, passion and distrust, reluctance and hope, ambition and creativity. She let him in, stripping away every barrier she had. And he was grateful for the gift.

Dev reached between their entwined bodies and found the hot warmth of her sex. He delved deep inside and relished the way her eyelids fluttered with the pleasure of his touch, but she wouldn't break the connection.

She let him see exactly what he was doing to her, hiding nothing.

Her body arched against his, searching. His own hips pumped against her belly, hard with a need only she could soothe. Her fingers tangled in the hair at his nape, tugging him backward so she could run the wicked edge of her tongue down his throat.

He growled deeply, the vibration of it echoing back to him through her hum of appreciation.

Grasping her leg, Dev hooked her knee around his arm and pushed her hips open wide. She was pink and swollen and perfect, and he couldn't deny himself any longer.

Driving deep, he slid home in one smooth stroke. Willow sighed as if her greatest wish had just been granted. The tight walls of her sex gripped him, urging him to give her more.

They rocked together, finding a rhythm that stole their breath. Dev's entire world narrowed to the woman beneath him. Her eyes were wild with desire, the answering need building steadily inside him.

He could feel the first quivers of her release, and still he drove them both harder, wanting to pull the last smidgen of pleasure from the moment. She bucked beneath him, meeting him thrust for thrust. And then her mouth was buried in his shoulder, her teeth gripping him as his skin absorbed her muffled scream.

And it was all he could take. The tingling started at the back of his thighs and rushed up to his spine, exploding out in the best orgasm he'd ever had. It ripped through him, stealing every sense from him but the feel of Willow wrapped tight around him.

His arms quivered as he tried to keep himself from crushing her completely, but Willow didn't seem to care. Her arms and legs were wrapped around him, holding him to her so that he could let go.

When he finally opened his eyes it was to find her watching him closely, a huge, satisfied smile stretching her swollen lips.

OVER THE NEXT couple of days they fell into a comfortable routine. Willow spent at least twelve hours holed up in her studio. Macey handled the boutique and rescheduled all appointments. The military bride had been fabulous, telling Willow that she'd love whatever dress she designed.

Even the country star had been less of a headache than Willow had anticipated. And the fact that she'd been sweet and very concerned actually made Willow want to do everything in her power to give the singer the dress of her dreams.

She'd called in anyone in town who could sew, and while letting go of the creative process was a little difficult, it was the only way they were going to repair the damage.

And Willow was determined to fix this.

Long after it had gone dark and the rest of her team had left, Dev would materialize in the doorway to her studio. Inevitably, he brought food and would coerce her into taking a break.

She slept little. What time she did take away from the studio was spent in Dev's arms. There was no question; she was burning the candle at both ends, but she couldn't stop. A pressure was building deep inside, a jittery awareness that left her feeling constantly on edge.

As if she was waiting for the other shoe to drop.

And maybe she was. The blog post, photograph, stalking and damage to her business were personal.

And since no one had a clue who was doing any of it, she was just waiting for something worse to happen.

Dev had been nothing but supportive, silently there for her whenever she'd needed him. Which actually only made her more uneasy. It was seductive, having him to lean on.

But he wouldn't always be there. Eventually he was going to have to return to the life he had outside Sweetheart, the one he'd been living for the past ten years. He had a business to run, friends, colleagues and employees who depended on him.

As much as she was enjoying this vacation from reality, it couldn't last. Dev had wormed his way into her bed, her life and, unfortunately, her soul. And while part of her wanted to paint little hearts around the situation—she had grown up in Sweetheart after all—she was smart enough to stop herself.

Devlin Warwick was going to leave her devastated—again—and there wasn't much she could do to stop it. At least, not now. It was too late.

But she wasn't ready to give him up, even if she knew she should. She hadn't felt this alive in a very long time. So she was walking on the wild side, knowing full well that eventually she'd have to pay the price for dancing with the devil.

There was no way for her to know just how high the cost would be.

It was late, well past midnight. She'd convinced Dev to go home without her after they'd shared the burgers he'd brought from the diner. She was so close to finishing the country star's dress that she'd wanted to plow through.

Unfortunately, the relief she felt staring at the finished product was short-lived.

A loud knock sounded on the studio door, making her jump. After everything that had happened, she'd taken to locking it.

Before she could ask who the heck was on the other side at this time of night, Hope's voice called through the barrier. "Willow, let us in."

"Us?" she asked, already crossing to flip the lock.

Pulling open the door, she stared at her friends crowded around—Hope, Lexi and Tatum. The grim expressions on their faces had her heart flip-flopping inside her chest.

"What's wrong?"

No one answered her. Instead, the three of them crossed to her worktable, cleared off the crystals, scraps and lace she hadn't had time to tidy up, and placed a laptop on the surface, opening it.

She glanced at each of them, searching for some clue as to what was coming, but there wasn't one.

Colors blinked to life. Words formed. And Willow's world fell apart.

Devlin Warwick Commits Adultery Again screamed at her in bold, black letters, taking up half the screen. Willow's stomach rolled and bile rose up her throat. But she kept reading.

According to the information, Dev had been married to a woman named Natalie Ford for the past eight years. There was even a picture of his marriage license with the bold slash of his handwriting clearly identifiable. At least, to anyone who knew him well. To her.

"How? What...?" Thoughts were racing around inside her head so fast she couldn't grab on to them. How could she not know that he was married? He didn't wear a ring, not even the pale band of one recently removed.

And then a memory flashed across her brain. That night. In her kitchen. The name of the woman who'd called him was Natalie.

The bastard had gone straight from sex with her to talking to his damn wife. And he hadn't even blinked.

Part of Willow wanted to be awed by his audacity. It took a hell of a lot of balls to do something like that with calm, cool indifference. But she was just pissed. Hurt. Betrayed beyond words.

God, she was an idiot. He'd used her. Taken the opportunity to get a taste of what circumstances had denied him ten years ago. He'd picked up the pieces and finished the game they'd been playing back then, finally getting what he wanted. Her.

And she'd let him. She'd made it easy, barely putting up a fight. Not even after the masks were off. She'd practically fallen into his bed, panting and begging.

Devlin Warwick had pulled her right down into the dirt with him. Rose might have screwed up his life—if he'd even told her the truth about that—but he'd managed to return the favor in spades. Only this time it was her life falling to pieces.

Willow groaned, dropping her head against the back of the chair. What was everyone going to think? She could just imagine the looks she was going to get. Disappointment. Horror. Disgust.

And she'd deserve every veiled glare and whisper. This is what happened when good girls did bad things—

like picking up a masked stranger at a party and letting him take her to bed.

Unfortunately, knowing that didn't stop it from hurting.

She'd believed him. Trusted him. Fallen in love with him.

And the whole time he was lying to her. Playing with her. Feeding her whatever lines he had to in order to get into her expensive panties.

Tears collected at the corners of her lashes. She tried to hold them back but couldn't quite manage it.

Her chest ached, as if someone was slowly crushing her.

She'd survived his betrayal once before. She wasn't sure she could do it again.

Back then she'd thought she loved him. But it had been the soft, idealistic, fairy-tale infatuation of youth. She hadn't really known him or understood who he was.

This time, she saw beneath the dark, indifferent mask he showed the world. Even as he'd lied, he'd let her see. Let himself be vulnerable.

And maybe that's what hurt the worst. With his words and his mouth and his eyes he'd convinced her to let go. To trust her body instead of her head. To take a leap with him.

Just so he could watch her fall.

13

"I'M TRYING REALLY hard not to think of you as a bastard right now, Warwick. I'm seriously hoping there's a decent explanation for what's going on."

Brett Newcomb's harsh voice rang through Dev's ears, but his brain was still half asleep and unable to process what the man was talking about.

Waiting for Willow to come home, he'd settled onto the sofa with his laptop to catch up some design work for another project they were bidding on. Apparently, he'd fallen asleep on the sofa. The loud burst of his cell phone had vaulted him out of a fitful sleep.

Dev scrubbed a hand down his face, trying to wake himself up. What few brain cells he did have functioning were busy spinning on why Willow wasn't home and not on whatever Brett was growling about. He was already pushing up from the sofa and searching for his keys so that he could drive down to the studio and check on her.

She'd told him she'd only be a couple more hours and that was at nine. It was now past midnight.

But Brett's next words stopped him midstride. "You're married."

Panic hit him hard, churning deep in his belly. "How do you know that?"

"So you don't deny it?"

Oh, shit. If Brett Newcomb knew then Willow did. He had to find her. Explain.

"Dammit!"

"Not the response I was looking for, asshole."

"Where is she?"

"I'm not telling you a damn thing."

Dev didn't have time to argue with Newcomb, he'd worry about repairing that relationship later. Right now he couldn't care less about the Consortium job. He needed to find Willow.

And the most logical place to start was her studio.

Not even bothering to grab a jacket, Dev raced to his truck and tore down the street, not caring if he woke the entire neighborhood.

He skidded into the parking lot, part of him relieved to find several cars there, including Willow's. Although that meant she wasn't alone and that he'd probably have to get through her friends first.

The door to her studio was standing wide-open. Willow sat in a chair, staring at a computer screen. Three of her friends surrounded her, their posture and expressions protective as they glared at him.

"You need to leave," one of them said. The two others shifted, blocking Willow behind them.

"Willow. Let me explain."

The chair beneath her squeaked as she shifted. In

the small gap between her two friends he could see a single pale blue eye.

He stared at her, begging with his eyes even as he tried to find the right words to make her listen.

"It's okay," she said, her voice low and scratchy. Regret twisted through him. He'd done that to her. Made her hurt. And he hated himself for it, but there was nothing he could do now but try to fix it.

One of her friends looked down at her, sympathy and affection in her expression. "Are you sure? We'll make him leave if you want."

"No. I need to hear what he has to say."

The resignation and finality in her words made his heart sink.

Slowly, the three women filed passed him, their daggered glares probably meant to hurt him. But he didn't care what any of them thought. He only cared what Willow thought.

"We'll be right outside."

"Gage and Brett could be here in less than five minutes if you need them."

A weak smile touched Willow's lips. "I don't think so. I know how both of your men respond to threats, and beating the shit out of him won't solve anything."

"Maybe not, but it'd make me feel better," one of them said, cracking her knuckles in a way that told him she was no stranger to defending herself.

When they were finally alone, Dev cleared his throat and swallowed. Stalling while he tried to find the right words that would make everything okay.

Until this moment—the imminent possibility that he

was going to lose Willow—he hadn't realized just how much he needed her. Cared about her.

"Is it true?"

He wet his lips and prayed. "Yes, technically I'm still married, but it's a mistake."

"You better believe it is."

"No, that's not what I mean."

He walked closer, trying to gauge whether she was truly listening with an open mind or if she'd already convicted him of the crime she thought he'd committed.

And that's really what he was afraid of. Was this ten years ago all over again? Would she believe the worst of him no matter what he said? Would she throw him out just like his grandfather had done?

"Until a few months ago Natalie and I both thought we'd been divorced for six years. Our paperwork got screwed up and we only found out about it when she filed for a new marriage license. We're fixing it."

Dev waited, his lungs burning with the need for oxygen, his body unable to do anything but watch for some sign of Willow's reaction.

Silence stretched between them. Her eyes bored into his. Her skin blanched pale and then flooded with color again.

Slowly, her tongue swiped across her bottom lip, leaving a slick trail that even now his body wanted him to lean in and taste.

"Why didn't you tell me?"

"You believe me?"

She swallowed, the long column of her throat working, and then she nodded.

All the tension leaked out of his body. He closed his

eyes and blew out the breath that had been stuck. Thank God. Finally, someone believed him.

But when he opened his eyes again the tears glistening in hers had it all rushing back.

"Why didn't you tell me?" she asked again and he realized he wasn't completely out of the woods yet.

"Because at first I didn't think it mattered. Natalie's been my ex-wife for years, Willow. The piece of paper we're missing is a legality and nothing more. Our marriage was a mistake we both made when we were too stupid and young to realize what we were doing. I don't think about it—or her—and sure as hell not when I'm with you."

Her mouth twisted. "Thanks for that, at least."

"What's that supposed to mean?"

"She called you. The other night. I was naked in your lap and you picked me up, put me down and walked away to answer her call."

Dev's mouth opened and closed but no sound came out. He wanted to ask her how she knew that, but had enough brain power to realize that was a quick way to get his ass kicked…and she wouldn't even need the help of the muscle waiting in the wings.

"I've only spoken to Natalie through our lawyer for years. Until a few months ago I didn't even know how to get in touch with her, but she insisted our lawyer give her my number. I was shocked when her name popped up on my phone, Willow. I was afraid something had happened."

"What did she want?"

"The address of a mutual friend for her wedding invitations."

Willow stared at him for several seconds and then a burst of laughter escaped from her parted lips. And just kept going. She dissolved into it, letting her head drop down onto her crossed arms even as her sides heaved with the need for air.

Dev stared at her, unsure exactly what to do or say. Finally, she raised her head, looking at him through the sheen of laughter and tears.

"Seriously. She wanted an address for wedding invitations?" Her voice quivered at the word *wedding,* as if she was in danger of melting into mad laughter again.

Eventually, she found solid ground and the laughter disappeared as quickly as it had come.

She looked up at him and something shifted. A shield he hadn't seen her wear since that night in the alley slipped back down. Instead of his passionate lover, the cool, reserved businesswoman sat in front of him.

Alarm jittered through him. "I thought you said you believed me."

"I do." Her voice went soft, full of an apology he didn't want. "But I'm not sure it really matters."

"What do you mean? Of course it matters."

"We both knew this couldn't last. It was heady and dangerous. A return to a past we both needed to put to rest."

Anger boiled inside him, pushing away the anxiety he didn't want to recognize. "That's bullshit."

"Dev, you make me do things I wouldn't normally do. Break my own rules. I can't keep acting this way. There are consequences. My business has been ransacked and my reputation left in tatters. And for what? Stellar sex?"

A sickening knot formed in the pit of his belly. She was pushing him away. Telling him to get lost. That he wasn't good enough for her precious, perfect life.

He stared at her and felt his throat begin to close. Emotions he thought had been long buried—insecurity, doubt, misery—reared up inside. Immediately he was that little boy everyone dismissed and judged. The rebellious teenager expected to fail. The young man his own grandfather hadn't even wanted around.

Everything inside him began to shut down, the familiar numbness of the protective wall seeping in.

No. He ground his teeth together and clenched his fists at his sides.

He would not let anyone, not even Willow, take his self-respect. He'd fought too hard to win it back, to find his place in the world. Where he belonged and what he was good at.

He had a successful business and a good education. He'd fought tooth and nail for everything and was grateful for the struggle because it meant he appreciated what he had.

Willow Portis didn't want him in her life. Fine. He refused to stay where he wasn't wanted. Or beg. He'd survived the damage one Portis sister had done, surely he could survive the other.

FOUR DAYS LATER, back in his life in Atlanta, he was failing miserably. Until he'd walked away from Willow, he would have said that nothing could have been more painful than leaving Sweetheart the first time.

He'd have been wrong.

And it wasn't just about Willow. Somehow the entire damn town had wormed its way back into his good graces. He missed the place. The nosy busybodies who'd stopped him on the street to threaten him about hurting Willow. Knowing everyone.

Hell, he'd lived in his house for four years and didn't even know his neighbors' names. And until two weeks ago that hadn't bothered him. It did now.

The pub, the diner, that damn club and the sense of belonging he hadn't wanted to feel but couldn't stop.

Everyone in his office was walking on eggshells. He knew they were talking behind his back, speculating about what had happened in Sweetheart to leave him prowling the hallways like a wounded bear.

Today he'd barked at Gladys, the sixty-year-old grandmother he'd hired to answer his phones. Everyone loved Gladys. She baked chocolate chip cookies for the office every Friday.

Her eyes had gone steely and her mouth had thinned, but she hadn't reprimanded him even though he'd definitely deserved it. He'd growled an apology at her, feeling guilty that he hadn't been able to manage anything more. He'd give her an extra day off instead.

It had been easy to bury himself in work, throwing all of his focus at the projects and bids he'd neglected while he was out of town. He had plenty of competent people to handle most of it, although if he didn't cool it he was going to lose all of them.

Pushing himself to the point of exhaustion so that he could fall into bed and shut off his mind was one thing. Demanding his employees act like they didn't have lives outside the office was another.

He'd founded the company on family values and insisted on flexibility. Not just because it was the right thing to do, but because when employees knew their families were taken care of, their time at the office was more productive.

Just because he didn't have anyone to go home to didn't mean no one else did.

A pain lanced through his chest. Dev tried to ignore it, but found himself rubbing a hand across his sternum anyway.

Pushing up from the sofa, he crossed to his fridge and grabbed a beer. While he'd been able to hold everything back so far, the weekend loomed huge and lonely in front of him.

Maybe he'd get drunk tonight and then visit the local Habitat for Humanity project he was helping sponsor tomorrow. If they weren't ready for him to start on the landscaping they could always use a pair of steady hands elsewhere. Backbreaking, mindless work was exactly what he needed.

But before he could put the first step of his plan into action, his cell phone rang. A bubble of hope burst in his chest before he managed to tamp it down.

If Willow had wanted to talk to him she would have already called. That didn't stop him from looking at the screen. And then groaning when he realized the call was from his ex-wife.

He'd spoken to the woman more in the past month than he had in six years. He couldn't ignore her, though.

"Natalie," he answered.

"Dev," she chirped, her voice bubbly and full of happiness.

Part of him wanted to resent the hell out of her for it.

But he couldn't do that, either. While it had been a long time since he'd been in love with her, he still wanted her to be happy.

"Did you hear? The final decree came through today. We're officially divorced."

"Beautiful," he grumbled, tacking on, "about four days too late," under his breath.

But she heard him anyway. "What do you mean four days too late?"

"Nothing."

"Don't do that," she scolded. "I always hated it when you did that. Dangle a tiny piece of information that I knew meant so much more than what was on the surface and then refuse to follow it up with the rest."

"I don't do that."

"Yes, you do. And it's annoying."

Dev sighed, closing his eyes and searching for some center of peace that he wasn't sure existed anymore. He might not have spoken to his ex-wife much over the years, but he hadn't forgotten just how tenacious she could be when she wanted something.

He could either answer her or live with her incessant pestering until she uncovered whatever it was.

"Fine. I met someone. She found out we were still married and told me to get lost."

Natalie sniffed. "If she wasn't willing to wait for you to get the divorce finalized then she wasn't worth your time."

He should keep his mouth shut and let her assume that the fault had been Willow's, but for some reason he couldn't do it.

"Well, I…uh…didn't tell her right away."

"Dev," Natalie groaned. He could practically see her eyes rolling with frustration. "What is wrong with you? If you were serious about her why wouldn't you tell her?"

"It's complicated. Willow and I have a history."

Silence buzzed down the line, for some reason making him restless. Dev stood and paced over to the windows that faced out onto his back garden.

"What kind of history?"

He shook his head, unhappy to be having this conversation with anyone, let alone his ex-wife. "It isn't important."

A heavy sigh gushed down the line at him. "You're doing it again, aren't you?"

"Doing what?"

"Pushing everyone away. Pretending that things are perfect when they aren't. Putting up the walls to keep people out."

He had no idea what she was talking about. "No."

Natalie scoffed. "I don't even have to ask if you care about her. Do you want to know why?"

Something told him he really didn't. The skin at the back of his neck tightened with apprehension. "Not particularly."

"I'm going to tell you anyway, sweetie. You run from anything that scares you."

His hands clenched into fists. "I do not." She was calling his masculinity into question.

"Pull back the porcupine quills. I'm not judging you. I do the same thing. Ask my fiancé. It's a defense mechanism, Dev, one you've developed honestly."

A dull roar began in the back of his head. Reaching

up, Dev tried to rub the relentless pounding away, but it didn't help. In that moment he would have given anything to shut Natalie up, but he didn't know what to say to stem the tide of words that had started.

"Everyone in your life has hurt you. Your mom, your dad, your grandfather, even me. Everyone you trusted and depended on let you down. The minute you feel yourself letting anyone in, you shut down. I should know. I spent two years banging my head against the walls you put up. Every time I thought I'd made a crack that I could wiggle through somehow you found another way to shut me out.

"I cared about you, Dev. Still do. But no matter what I did you wouldn't let me in. And I got tired of fighting. It was easier to walk away, and the fact that you let me told me I'd made the right decision."

Dev opened his mouth to argue with her, to tell her that the only reason he'd let her go was because that's what she'd wanted. But he couldn't make the words form. Because they weren't true.

He'd been relieved when Natalie had told him she was taking a job in California and that she was going alone.

"I'm sorry" was all he could manage.

"Don't be," she said, her sweet voice breezy with dismissal. "I'm not. We would have made each other miserable and I knew that no matter how unhappy you got you'd never leave. Not only did you make a vow to me, but there was no way you'd walk away from a family, even if it was the right thing to do."

Jesus, she made him sound like a masochistic prick. "I didn't mean to hurt—"

She cut him off. "You didn't. You might have cared about me, but you obviously love this woman."

The protest was on his lips before he could form the thought, "No, I—"

Again, she interrupted, refusing to let him get the words out. "I can hear it in your voice, Dev. The kind of longing that was never there between us. I know because I've found it, too."

"I'm glad." And he genuinely was. Natalie was sweet and giving, bubbly and open. But she didn't make his blood sing. Never had.

That was something he'd only ever found with Willow.

"I'm going to give you some friendly advice. Consider it a parting gift. Go to her. Find a way to work out whatever's wrong. Grovel. Buy her diamonds. Tell her your deepest, darkest secrets. Whatever it takes."

"She told me to leave."

"And you did it, no doubt with barely a glance on your way out. Better to leave before she hurt you more. You deserve to be happy, Dev, but you've got to be willing to fight for it."

Every muscle in his body bunched tight. The hard edge of his cell bit into his palm.

With very little help, he'd dragged himself out of the gutter. He'd worked his ass off for everything he had and didn't regret a single moment.

Every struggle had taught him something.

But that had been easy. Hard work was never anything he'd been afraid of. Opening himself up...now that was another thing.

It had been a long time since he'd bothered to fight

for someone to love him. When he was young he'd tried. He remembered making sandwiches for his hungover mother, hoping that the gesture would make her happy. Make her wake up and pay attention to him…if only for a little while. But no matter what he'd done, the drugs were always more important to her.

When his grandfather had gotten so angry…had he really tried as hard as he could to convince him of the truth? No, he'd accepted the anger and disappointment because that's what he'd come to expect. What he knew how to deal with.

He hadn't argued with Natalie or tried to convince her not to take the job. Or that he could go with her. He'd just let her walk away.

And he was doing it again with Willow, silently accepting that he wasn't good enough for her. Ten years ago he might have been right, but not anymore.

Almost before the thought was formed, he was racing for his truck, the red monstrosity pointed straight for home.

14

DEV WAS GONE. And she was devastated. But she had no one to blame but herself.

For days she'd gone through the motions. Everywhere she went the soft rustling of whispers followed. She hadn't bothered to tell anyone the truth. Not because she didn't believe Dev, but because it was none of their damn business.

That didn't stop people from talking. And staring at her with hard questions in their eyes. For the first time in her life, Willow understood how Rose must have felt those last months before she moved away— under a microscope, her life open for public discussion.

The difference was that Rose had signed up for that response, had invited it every time she walked out of the house in skintight clothes and stumbled down Main Street drunk. She'd solicited the scrutiny, and looking back Willow realized, reveled in it.

Dev had been right. Rose was exactly where she wanted to be, beneath the spotlight in Vegas.

But unlike Rose, Willow had done nothing wrong. And neither had Dev.

More than protecting her own image, she'd come close to putting some gossiping busybody in her place a couple times on Dev's behalf. He'd lost so much because of Rose's lie. It bothered her to realize it was easy for everyone in town to believe the worst of him. But she'd bitten her tongue and hated herself for letting her own fear and weakness make her no better than anyone else.

She'd let him go. Not because she hadn't believed him, but because the moment had given her the escape she'd desperately needed. The longer she spent with Dev, the more panicked she became. The harder she fell for him, the more damage losing him was going to do.

But not even knowing she'd made the right choice seemed to stem the pain. It hurt, but the fact that Dev had disappeared proved that she'd made the right decision.

He'd walked away from her without a second glance.

Two days later a For Sale sign had sprung up on the lawn of his grandfather's house.

How could a piece of cardboard and metal hurt so much?

But she hadn't had time to stop and crumble. The Nashville princess had shown up that same day for her final fitting. The dress wasn't exactly what she'd ordered, but it was better. And the glowing expression on her face when she slipped it on told Willow the bride agreed. She looked amazing in the creation and Willow was almost grateful to whoever had broken in and destroyed the first dress.

This design would get her noticed—in a good way.

Paparazzi, magazines and gossip sites would splash pictures of her dress everywhere. The positive press gave her something else to concentrate on.

The second bride's dress had been breathtaking. Perfect for her slender body, clinging to her curves in all the right places and letting hints of bare skin peek through at her back and shoulders. While Willow'd had to improvise on the intricate crystal design she'd wanted down the back, they'd both ended up pleased with the final result.

The mother and daughter had even invited her to the wedding. And while she appreciated the gesture, the last thing she wanted right now was to watch someone else walk down the aisle toward their happily-ever-after.

She wished the woman the best, but she just didn't have that in her right now. Not while her own life was falling to pieces.

Macey had insisted she take a few days off, telling her she'd earned the rest. But the inactivity was just driving her crazy. She was restless and achy. If she hadn't known better she would have thought she was coming down with something, but it wasn't her muscles or joints that hurt. It was the big gaping hole in the center of her chest.

And no over-the-counter drug could fix that.

She just needed time. And possibly a week on a white, sandy beach. But she couldn't make herself book the trip.

Even with all the hard stares and whispers, Sweetheart was home. Her friends were here and right now she needed them more than the healing heat of the sun.

What surprised Willow most in those few days was

realizing she didn't really care if everyone was talking about her and judging her choices. Somewhere between her teen years, when that had been her worst nightmare, and today she'd discovered there were more important things than public opinion. It was a revelation to discover she just didn't care what most people thought about her. And the ones who did matter had only sympathy and support to share.

Willow finally reached her breaking point and, disobeying a direct order, went into her studio. She'd hoped to find some comfort there, lose herself in the creative process.

But sitting at her worktable, staring at her blank sketchpad, nothing came. The only thing she could think about was the first night Dev had invaded her sanctuary. How he'd wandered around her space, his wide, masculine hands running softly across the feminine trappings of her job.

He should have stuck out, but instead he'd blended in. As if he belonged there. A heavy band squeezed tight across her chest, making it hard to breathe.

Willow wasn't sure how long she sat there, her mind spinning in unproductive circles, but a noise at the door finally pulled her out of the mental quicksand.

Startled, Willow jerked her gaze up to find Erica Condon standing just inside her workroom.

A frown creased the spot between her brows. "Erica, what are you doing here? How'd you get in?"

She'd been alone, slipping in after Macey had locked up the boutique for the night. Glancing at the clock on the wall she realized it was almost ten. How had she lost two hours sitting here?

Erica closed the door and leaned against it, her hands remaining locked around the knob.

"I'm good with locks." She shrugged, and a tiny frisson of alarm shot into Willow's system.

"It's a little late to be shopping, Erica. We're closed. But Macey will be here in the morning."

"I don't want a dress, certainly not one that you've designed."

Standing, Willow darted a glance around her. Coming to the studio had been a spur-of-the-moment decision. She'd grabbed her keys and phone and nothing more, but now she couldn't remember where she'd set them down.

Maybe they were buried beneath the scrap material piled on the table. Shifting slowly, she tried to put the wall of her body between Erica and the table so she could search surreptitiously.

She had no idea what was going on or what Erica wanted, but whatever it was couldn't be good. She'd been so caught up in the ravages of losing Dev that it had been easy to forget someone was stalking her, especially when nothing had happened since her workroom had been destroyed.

"Don't move," Erica's harsh voice slipped through the room.

Willow froze, realizing for the first time that the other woman held something black and slender in her hand. Cold panic rushed through her along with a burst of adrenaline when Erica raised the snubbed nose of a weapon in her direction.

It took several seconds to recognize that it wasn't a

gun. It was shaped like one, but the bright yellow markings down the side and across the front gave it away.

Not that the sucker wouldn't hurt her, Willow had no illusions about that. But at least she wouldn't die if Erica went off the deep end and shot her with the Taser.

A sickening smile twisted Erica's mouth. "A girl can never be too careful."

Willow nodded, silently agreeing. For the first time, she truly looked at Erica.

She knew the woman. Erica and Rose had been friends, and even if Willow was a few years behind, she'd met her when they were younger. Erica worked for Hope at the *Sentinel.* But there wasn't a single reason she could come up with for Erica to be pointing the business end of a Taser in her direction.

"You made him leave."

An unnatural gleam entered the other woman's dull brown eyes. If the weapon wasn't enough to tell Willow just how close to the edge she was, that look would have been.

How could anyone have missed that Erica was unhinged?

"Who? Made who leave?"

"Wick. You hurt him. Just like Rose. And he left."

Willow swallowed and shifted on her feet, trying to distract Erica while she resumed the search for her cell.

"I should have known you were just like your sister. Users, both of you. This time I tried to warn him, but he was blinded by lust and didn't want to listen."

Relief flooded Willow when her fingers finally brushed across the hard plastic edge of her phone, but it was short-lived. She couldn't exactly pull it in front of her to dial.

Knowing she needed to keep Erica talking, Willow asked, "What do you mean 'this time'?" as she tried to visualize the screen on her phone.

If she could just get it to dial someone, anyone, maybe they'd be able to hear what was going on and call for help.

Regret and guilt mixed with the manic glitter in Erica's eyes. "If I'd known what Rose was planning to do I would have stopped her. You have to believe me."

"I do," Willow reassured her.

Her fingers, slippery with fear, finally hit the right button. The soft buzz as a line opened and dialed came to her, faint enough that she was hopeful Erica couldn't hear.

"I was so angry with her when I realized, but it was too late. Everyone thought they'd slept together. Marcus went ballistic, threatening her and putting a hole through the wall next to her head. She called me, sobbing, and told me the truth about what she'd done."

Willow sucked in a hard breath. Rose had never mentioned what had happened the night Marcus found out.

"Wick left. Before I'd gotten up the courage to tell him I'd loved him for years." Pain twisted deep in Erica's eyes and for a moment Willow couldn't stop herself from feeling sorry for her.

And then the flash of vulnerability was gone, replaced by the hard edge of crazed anger.

"When I saw him at the masquerade I thought it was my second chance. Rose wasn't around, so maybe he'd notice me. But the moment you walked into that room with your skintight dress and those ridiculous angel wings he couldn't stop staring at you."

Disgust dripped from her words. "Just like Rose. What spell do you Portis women use to blind him?"

Willow shook her head, unsure what the safe answer to that question might be. Although Erica didn't appear to expect one.

"It doesn't matter. I won't let you hurt him anymore. Someone has to protect him, even from himself. Poor Wick, he has no one. Just like me."

Erica stepped closer. Willow wanted to move back, but she was pressed against the worktable and there was nowhere for her to go.

Without warning, the barbs shot out of the end of the gun and lodged in her body. A jolt of electricity shot through her with a sizzling pain that had her screaming in surprise and agony. She collapsed beneath the dead weight of her useless muscles.

The pain stopped. Every muscle in her body ached. She tried to pull a deep breath into her lungs.

Another jolt hit. Her body bowed against the burning torment. And then she blacked out.

SOMEWHERE BETWEEN ATLANTA and Sweetheart, Dev realized that he couldn't show up on Willow's doorstep in the middle of the night. Partly because he was afraid she'd just slam the door in his face.

So his plan was to head to his house, grab a little sleep and find a way to talk to her in the morning. The conversation was too important to run off half-cocked. He needed to stop and think. Make sure he knew exactly what to say to convince her they belonged together.

But that plan changed about twenty minutes outside town when his phone rang.

Grabbing it out of the cup holder, he glanced at the screen. Everything stilled and then his heart began thumping painfully in his chest.

He tried not to let any of the hope or restless uncertainty color his voice, but he didn't succeed very well. He answered, her name coming out almost as a groan. "Willow."

But she didn't speak.

"Willow?"

He was about to hang up, his heart plummeting into his stomach, when a muffled sound stopped him. Voices. They were faint at first, as if the phone had been covered by something but was suddenly free.

"When I saw him at the masquerade I thought it was my second chance. Rose wasn't around so maybe he'd notice me. But the moment you walked into that room with your skintight dress and those ridiculous angel wings he couldn't stop staring at you."

He didn't recognize the harsh, accusing voice, but he understood the words. And panic hit him full force.

Willow was in trouble. And she'd called him for help.

Dev's foot slammed the pedal to the floor. His truck lurched forward as gas and power flooded into the engine.

"Just like Rose. What spell do you Portis women use to blind him?"

God, he had no idea where she was. He should call the sheriff, but he didn't want to cut off the only lifeline he had to her in order to do it. Maybe she'd give him a clue. Anything.

He flashed past the sign into Sweetheart, uncaring that he was breaking several laws. He hoped Grant saw him. Please, God.

Helpless rage filled him. He slammed his fist against the steering wheel.

And then the worst sound he'd ever heard filled the cab. The high-pitched wail of Willow's scream. The phone clattered. And then it went dead.

Oh, hell. He was going to be too late.

No.

Almost crushing the phone in his fist, Dev somehow managed to speed dial the personal cell number Grant had given him several days ago.

He refused to lose her. Not when he'd just found her again.

15

GOD, HER HEAD HURT. Willow groaned and tried to curl her body into a ball. Everything hurt.

There was something wrong. She was in trouble. Alarm and confusion crashed down over her, flooding her body with a burst of adrenaline. She had to move. Get away. But she couldn't remember why.

A soft hand brushed against her forehead. She whimpered, not because it hurt but because it felt so good. Soothing. Safe.

Slowly, her eyes opened and she stared up into a dark blue gaze.

"Hang in there, angel. Help's on the way."

She nodded. Reality was seeping back in, a black-edged nightmare. Or maybe this was a dream.

No, her body hurt too much for that.

The hard floor pressed against her. Her head was cradled in Dev's lap. Rolling her eyes, she saw another pair of legs sticking out from beneath her worktable. Following the line of them, she realized they belonged to Erica

Condon, who was unconscious, her arms twisted behind her back and tied together with a white strip of material.

She licked her lips. "How?"

Dev bent down, pressed his lips against hers in the softest touch and whispered, "Shh."

Sirens wailed in the distance.

"I was already on my way back when I got your call."

She'd called him? She supposed it made sense since he was probably the last person she'd phoned. She hadn't exactly been in a chatty mood the past few days.

"You were already on your way back?"

Closing his eyes, Dev pressed his forehead to hers for several seconds before nodding.

"I love you, Willow. And I'm not willing to walk away. Or let you push me away. I'm going to stay and fight this time. Even if you don't want me to.

"I screwed up. I should have told you about Natalie, but I was afraid. When I came to Sweetheart, I thought what I was looking for was closure. A chance to put the past behind me and lay to rest the ghosts of my mistakes and bad choices."

He pulled away, that dark and dangerous gaze caressing her face. A shiver raced through her body.

"I came back for you."

His arms tightened around her, bands of hard muscle that made her feel safe. Her body relaxed, sinking into the comfort and security of him.

Circling her arms around his neck, Willow pulled him back down to her. Her words kissed his mouth. "Tell me again."

"What?"

"That you love me."

With a groan, he closed his eyes and brought them skin to skin. She enjoyed the gentle rasp of his stubble-roughened jaw against her cheek. "I love you so much it hurts," he promised.

Threading her fingers into the hair at his nape, Willow whispered, "I know. I was so afraid. You broke my heart once, and I wasn't sure I could live through it again."

"You don't have to. I'm not going anywhere."

"But what about your business? You have a life in Atlanta, Dev. And my studio is here."

"We'll figure it out."

"I could move to Atlanta."

"No." Dev shook his head, a stubborn glint shooting through his eyes.

"You hate Sweetheart."

The pad of his thumb slipped across her bottom lip. "No, I don't. You're here and that's all that matters. But, believe it or not, the place has kinda grown on me."

The wail increased. A sharp whine sounded as someone squealed into the alley at the back of the store.

He had just enough time to say, "We have plenty of time to figure out the details, Willow," and then people were flooding in the back door.

Sheriff Grant and two of his deputies. A couple of paramedics. Chaos swirled around her, but through it all Dev was right beside her, refusing to let her go.

DEV CRACKED OPEN Willow's bedroom door. Even as he worried about disturbing her, he couldn't stop himself. It had been difficult to let her out of his sight.

She'd scared the hell out of him and he wasn't sure

how quickly the need to reassure himself that she was fine would fade. Or if it ever would.

He'd lost so many people…the thought of losing her, too, still scared him. But not enough to let her go.

His eyes scanned the bed, surprised to find it empty. The covers were a rumpled pile, but Willow wasn't beneath them. A quick jolt of alarm shot through him as his eyes swept the room.

He found her standing in front of the wide windows facing out onto the street. Her arms were wrapped around her body and she stared, a sad, faraway expression on her face.

On quiet feet, he padded across the room, slipping his arms around her and pulling her back against his body.

She melted into his hold. Warmth crawled through him.

"Do you need one of the pain pills the doc gave you?"

She shook her head. "No, I'm fine. Just a little achy. Nothing some ibuprofen can't fix."

He stirred against her. "Let me get you some."

Her arms wrapped around his, locking him in place. "In a minute."

Her body was lax, her heat slipping through the thin nightgown and silk robe into him. But he could practically hear the wheels grinding together in her head.

"What's wrong?"

She sighed. "How did everyone miss it? Erica worked for Hope." Willow pointed out the window to the house down the street. "She lived right there for years. How did none of us know?"

A heavy weight settled in his chest. He hated that

anything ugly had touched Willow. She was so giving and protective.

Erica Condon had stalked her and attacked her, but that didn't stop her from worrying about the woman.

"She'd had years of practice hiding secrets. Grant said she broke down, years and years of suppressed anguish and resentment pouring out of her. She was emotionally and physically abused."

"How could we not know?" she asked again, sorrow filling her words.

"You aren't responsible for the world, Willow. She's going to get the help she needs. That's all we can do for her."

With gentle pressure, he turned her away from the window. Staring at Erica's house wasn't going to help her.

His hands slipped beneath the robe that she'd left open. He circled her waist, enjoying the soft glide of silk against skin.

God, he wanted her. He couldn't be this close to her and not want her. But she'd been through a lot in the past twenty-four hours and the last thing she needed was him pushing her.

So he pulled back, putting several precious inches between them. He searched her face, looking for signs of strain or pain. When he didn't find any, the constricting weight that had been sitting on his chest since he'd gotten that call finally began to ease.

"Are you hungry?"

Slowly, she nodded.

"Do you want me to make you something?"

The tip of her tongue swept out across her lips. His

gaze was pulled there. He was human, after all. Her lips were wet and tempting. His fingers tightened at her hips, trying to find a slippery hold on the control he was quickly losing.

"No," she said, taking a single step to close the gap. Her body pressed against him, soft curves meeting hard planes.

Her head tipped back so that she could look him square in the eyes. And what he saw there made him swallow.

"What do you want?" he asked, his voice gravelly with his need to touch her.

"You." Her simple answer drew a groan from deep in his belly.

With one last valiant effort at control, he tried to push her away. "I don't want to hurt you."

But she wouldn't let him. Rolling up onto her toes, she brought their mouths together. "You won't. I trust you, Dev. I need you. Please."

He couldn't refuse her anything, least of all something he wanted just as desperately.

Picking her up, he brought them together. Her legs wrapped tight around his waist and she clung to him. Her eyes filled with passion and he felt the answering heat building deep inside.

She was beautiful, her dark hair a cloud around her face. The robe slipped from her shoulders, falling to the floor in a puddle. Her skin was pale and soft.

He buried his face in the crook of her neck, his mouth finding her. Her scent, honeysuckle and Willow, filled him.

She grabbed on to his hair, tugging until he looked up at her.

She was his. Finally. His own angel. He loved her, tarnished halo and all. She knew everything. Saw straight through him. And still wanted him. Loved him. Accepted him, flaws and all.

Dev had no idea what he'd done to deserve her, but he had every intention of appreciating the gift he'd been given.

Turning, he placed her in the center of the bed. He started at the curve of her foot and trailed his mouth upward. Soft, worshipping kisses. She writhed beneath him, panting.

"You're killing me," she ground out against the building fever.

His lips curved against her skin. "I don't think anyone's ever died from delayed gratification."

Her hands fisted in his hair, pulling his mouth to hers. "You really are a devil."

"Yeah, angel, but you love me."

Willow pulled away, putting several inches between them so she could stare straight into his eyes, into his soul. And she let him see all of her.

In that moment there were no masks. No disguises. No walls or barriers or past between them. More than just skin to skin, they were naked. And he'd never loved her more.

It had taken them ten years, but they'd finally found each other again. And he had no intention of ever letting her go.

* * * * *

REQUEST YOUR FREE BOOKS!
2 FREE NOVELS PLUS 2 FREE GIFTS!

red-hot reads!

YES! Please send me 2 FREE Harlequin® Blaze™ novels and my 2 FREE gifts (gifts are worth about $10). After receiving them, if I don't wish to receive any more books, I can return the shipping statement marked "cancel." If I don't cancel, I will receive 4 brand-new novels every month and be billed just $4.74 per book in the U.S. or $4.96 per book in Canada. That's a savings of at least 14% off the cover price. It's quite a bargain. Shipping and handling is just 50¢ per book in the U.S. and 75¢ per book in Canada.* I understand that accepting the 2 free books and gifts places me under no obligation to buy anything. I can always return a shipment and cancel at any time. Even if I never buy another book, the two free books and gifts are mine to keep forever.

150/350 HDN F4WC

Name	(PLEASE PRINT)

Address	Apt. #

City	State/Prov.	Zip/Postal Code

Signature (if under 18, a parent or guardian must sign)

Mail to the **Harlequin® Reader Service:**
IN U.S.A.: P.O. Box 1867, Buffalo, NY 14240-1867
IN CANADA: P.O. Box 609, Fort Erie, Ontario L2A 5X3

Want to try two free books from another line?
Call 1-800-873-8635 or visit www.ReaderService.com.

* Terms and prices subject to change without notice. Prices do not include applicable taxes. Sales tax applicable in N.Y. Canadian residents will be charged applicable taxes. Offer not valid in Quebec. This offer is limited to one order per household. Not valid for current subscribers to Harlequin Blaze books. All orders subject to credit approval. Credit or debit balances in a customer's account(s) may be offset by any other outstanding balance owed by or to the customer. Please allow 4 to 6 weeks for delivery. Offer available while quantities last.

Your Privacy—The Harlequin® Reader Service is committed to protecting your privacy. Our Privacy Policy is available online at www.ReaderService.com or upon request from the Harlequin Reader Service.

We make a portion of our mailing list available to reputable third parties that offer products we believe may interest you. If you prefer that we not exchange your name with third parties, or if you wish to clarify or modify your communication preferences, please visit us at www.ReaderService.com/consumerschoice or write to us at Harlequin Reader Service Preference Service, P.O. Box 9062, Buffalo, NY 14269. Include your complete name and address.

HB13R

Lying in Your Arms

Leo checked out the rest of the room, pausing in the bath-
room to strip out of his clothes and grab a towel, which he
slung over one shoulder. He returned to the patio door, put
one hand on the jamb and another on the slider, and stood
naked in the opening, letting that tropical breeze bathe his
body in coolness.

Heaven.

He was just about to step outside and let the warm late-day
sun soak into his skin when he heard something very out of
place. A voice. A woman's voice. Coming from right behind
him…inside his room.

"Oh. My. God!"

Shocked, he swung around, instinctively yanking the towel
off his shoulder.

A woman stood in his room, staring at him, wide-eyed. They
stared at each other, silent, surprised, and Leo immediately
noticed several things about her.

She was young—his age, maybe. Definitely not thirty.

She was uncomfortable, tired or not feeling well. Her
blouse clung to her curvy body, as it was moist with sweat.

Dark smudges cupped her red-rimmed eyes, and she'd already kicked off her shoes, which rested on the floor right by the door, as if her first desire was to get barefoot, pronto.

Oh. And she was hot. Jesus, was she ever.

She was one more thing, he suddenly realized.

Shocked. Stunned. Maybe a little afraid.

"Hi," he said with a small smile. He remained where he was, not wanting to startle her.

Her green eyes moved as she shifted her attention over his body, from bare shoulders, down his chest, then toward the white towel that he clutched in his fist right at his belly. Finally, something like comprehension washed over her face.

"Look, I don't know who put you up to this, but I don't need you."

"Don't need me for what?" *To do your taxes? Cut your hair? Carry your suitcase?*

Put out your fire?

Oh, he suspected he could do that last one, and it wasn't just because of his job.

"To have sex with me."

His jaw fell open. *"What?"*

She licked her lips. "I mean, you're very attractive and all." Her gaze dropped again. "Still, I think you'd better get out."

"I can't do that," he said, his voice low, thick.

He edged closer, unable to resist lifting a hand to brush a long, drooping curl back from her face, tucking it behind her ear.

"Why not?" she whispered.

"Because you're in my room."

**Pick up LYING IN YOUR ARMS by Leslie Kelly,
on sale September 17, 2013,
wherever Harlequin® Blaze® books are sold.**

Mission: Keep Margaret Barlow distracted...using any means necessary!

All professor Maggie Barlow wanted was a night of wicked satisfaction from the dead-sexy ranger, Hunter Cross. Having him as her official army liaison while she works on her new book? That *wasn't* in the plan. Especially when she learns that Hunter has orders to "control" her. Little does the army know that when it comes to their deliciously naughty nighttime activities, Hunter is at Maggie's complete command....

Pick up

Command Performance

by *Sara Jane Stone,*

available September 17, 2013, wherever you buy Harlequin Blaze books.

HARLEQUIN®

Blaze®

Red-Hot Reads

www.Harlequin.com

Love the Harlequin book you just read?

Your opinion matters.

Review this book on your favorite book site, review site, blog or your own social media properties and share your opinion with other readers!

Be sure to connect with us at:
Harlequin.com/Newsletters
Facebook.com/HarlequinBooks
Twitter.com/HarlequinBooks

HARLEQUIN®

A Romance FOR EVERY MOOD™

**Stay up-to-date on all your
romance-reading news with the
Harlequin Shopping Guide,
featuring bestselling authors, exciting new
miniseries, books to watch and more!**

The newest issue will be delivered right to you
with our compliments! There are 4 each year.

Signing up is easy.

EMAIL

ShoppingGuide@Harlequin.ca

WRITE TO US

HARLEQUIN BOOKS
Attention: Customer Service Department
P.O. Box 9057, Buffalo, NY 14269-9057

OR PHONE

1-800-873-8635 in the United States
1-888-343-9777 in Canada

Please allow 4-6 weeks for delivery of the first issue by mail.